SUGAR AND ICE

Arizona Raptors, book 4

RJ SCOTT
V.L. LOCEY

Love Lane Books

Copyright

All Rights Reserved

Dedication

For Kelly E Lipp who named Vlad's parrot Frank.

---

*To my family who accepts me and all my foibles and
quirks. Even the plastic banana in my holster.*
VL Locey

Always for my family.
RJ Scott

SUGAR and ICE

RJ SCOTT & V.L. LOCEY

Chapter One

Tate

MY CANCELLED WEDDING DAY PASSED IN A BLUR. I WAS drunk, obliterated, because I'd woken up this morning and decided it was the only way I could deal with the shit storm that was my life.

I knew I was at home, that was where the drinking had started, and I knew for sure both my brother and sister were there, but the rest was a haze of not caring what the hell I was doing, and reveling in breaking all the goddamn rules that guided my life.

Be nice to people. Always be nice. Don't be a dick. Don't let the money go to your head. Play the best hockey you can. Don't fuck up. And mostly don't fuck guys.

No one had told me the one about not hooking up with Lacey, my psychotic, murderous, cat-stealing, ex-fiancée.

Where was that in the how-to-be-a-perfect-hockey-professional rule book?

"IblimissaObi," I slurred, and felt my sister's arm on

my shoulder. I did miss my cat, Obi, he was a good cat, a Maine Coon who was all fur and big woobly eyes, and he loved me.

Lacey wouldn't let me take him when I left.

I could've bought a million cats if I'd wanted, maybe two, but it was Obi I wanted right now, all curled up in my lap, or riding around on my shoulder. Obi was my friend.

My best friend.

My only friend.

"LeeblissaObi," I repeated some jumbled up mess of words.

"We know you do, little brother," Josie murmured.

I tumbled sideways into her, but I must have misjudged because I sprawled onto my huge-ass sectional in my huge-ass front room, in my freaking empty-as-fuck mansion. I lived close to a singer whose name I'd forgotten but who'd won some show and did Insta shit, and opposite a championship boxer who was all bling and very little conversation, other than muted grunts. Millionaires' row, exactly where I belonged with my twenty-million something sign-up to the Arizona something or other. I belonged here. Obi my beautiful Maine Coon belonged here with me, not down in Dallas with Lacey and her acid tongue, and her interviews, and her big eyes dripping tears on daytime talk shows.

Did he ever hurt you? they asked her, and fuck me if she just shook her head a little whilst dramatically looking down and left. People drew their own conclusions, Tate Collins, the Captain America of Hockey had hurt this cute, sweet young woman who loved cats.

My cat!

And then Dallas had told me to get the fuck out, they'd expected more of me, they'd told me *things*, vital things, and I'd told Lacey and now *things* were out there for everyone to know. Lies. It was all lies, but no one believed me. Not even the freaking Raptors with their rainbow shit, and their crappy games, and the fact that no one on the team liked me.

"FuckemRaptors," I slurred, and snapped my fingers, sliding off the sofa and onto the thick white carpet, leaning to one side and then flailing as I ended up lying flat on my back.

"Jesus!" The voice was far away. Far *far* away, like a million billion miles from me. "What the fuck, Tot?"

"G'way!"

"Have you got him? Get his other arm… 911?"

911? Wasn't that a television show? With like all these heroes doing hero shit and rescuing people? Important dudes who deserved to be called heroes. Not messed-up idiot hockey players who just play a game.

"He'll kill us if we call—"

"Phnargle shump," I blurted, which totally made sense in my head, telling whoever was here that I didn't need the paramedics, because that would shatter any illusions left about the perfect guy everyone bought into.

"What did he say?"

"Hell if I know."

I twisted to stand and smacked my head on something hard, and I opened one eye. Why was there a toilet in my front room?

Wait? The floor is hard. Where was the carpet? I wanted my carpet back. I gripped the porcelain, felt sick, lost whatever was in my stomach, which was basically any alcohol I had in the house, from vodka to alcopops, plus as many packets of the shittiest snacks that Josie had left on her last visit.

"Ja-hossseeeeeee," I managed.

"S'okay, Tot, we got you," Josie reassured.

"We have?" The second voice, decidedly male, belonged to my big brother Logan, who levered me to stand, and then I was wet. It was raining in my bathroom, tropically raining in a rainy kind of way, with pulses as if the clouds were squeezing themselves. I was so wet that I wish I wasn't in my clothes, only… I was naked, no clothes, nothing, and was Josie in the room?

"Jo'eee cock." I scrambled to cover myself but whoever was holding me up sniggered, and then slathered something that smelled of oranges all over me. I hoped to hell it was Logan; it sure sounded like Logan.

"She's gone," Logan reassured me. "It's just you and me, Tot, and you stink."

I opened the other eye, which wasn't working, then realized I'd actually shut the first one, and I tried my hardest to open both, wanting to cry because this was my wedding day and I was in the shower with my brother who was supposed to be my best man, Logan. He was wiping sick and shit and holding me up, and Josie was out there probably crying or something that would break my heart, because she was my sister and she was everything to me.

"Love you," I put all my attention into forming the words clearly, and they didn't sound bad, echoing, and a little loud, but they made sense.

"Love you too, Tot, now wash your ass."

I tried, I really did, but he had to hold me up, and I felt as legless as a newborn kitten. No, not legless, kittens had legs. Some didn't, though. I felt tears push up past the bile thinking about all the lost and lonely kittens who didn't have legs.

"Imma gonna 'dopt legless kittens," I managed.

"Okay, okay, come on, let's get this soap off."

"Gonna call Bob, he'll get me legless kittens in a bucket…" That didn't sound right. "No, bucket load."

"Your agent is the best person to get you kittens," Logan lied. I knew he was lying. He hated Bob. Said that Bob only stayed after the shit hit the fan in Dallas because of my money. Of course he did.

All people wanted from me was money.

Logan rinsed me off, and some of the water went into my mouth, and I needed that, warm water that quenched my thirst.

"Nomorebeer," I managed.

"We got this."

"Kittens though."

"All the kittens, Tot, all of them."

I wished my big brother wouldn't call me Tot now that I was super-old, but then I wished he wasn't holding me up in a shower, and I was glad of both at the same time. Somehow he got me out of the shower, and then wrapped me in fluffy, soft towels, and the caring and gentle words he used cut through my drinking pity party for one. I gripped his shirt, finally opening both eyes, nausea dragging at every cell of me, and looked at Logan. Emotion welled, maybe it was the kittens, or the love he showed me, or the way he called me Tot. Maybe it was because today was supposed to be the day I married Lacey, and I'd never loved her, and this was all my fault.

Whatever it was, my emotions began spilling in tears and curses and being sick again, only this time Josie stroked my head, Logan held me, and neither of them moved away. We ended up on the sofa, Logan forcing me to drink blue water with electrolytes, my favorite, and Josie stroking my head and telling me I'd be okay. Slowly, the stupid, self-pitying, emotional, life-ending tears subsided, and the cursing stopped, and the intense reaction to today's date subsided one teeny tiny legless kitten at a time.

"I don't understand what happened," I said.

Logan sighed. "You see, Tot, the way this works is that you drink the alcohol, and your body—"

"I meant with Lacey. I know she's had issues with her mental health, but I thought… I really thought that she loved me."

"I know, Tot."

"And I thought that I loved her."

"Let's get you to bed," Logan murmured, and helped me stand.

Somehow he and Josie managed to get me to my room, which was bigger than our entire house had been when we were kids, and they helped me into my bed, with its billion thread count whatever, and the pillows that were as gentle and soft as clouds. The room was spinning, but I closed my eyes.

"There's water here, Advil, and a bucket, and we'll be outside."

And I think I must have slept, and I only recall being sick once more.

WHEN I CRACKED OPEN AN EYE I REACHED BLINDLY FOR the bottle of water and Advil that Logan had left me and swallowed enough that I hoped this headache would leave me the hell alone.

What had I done?

I'd woken to a hundred regrets, and none of them made any sense this morning. I managed to get up and out of bed, the cool air of the room hitting my naked everything.

Shit. Had Josie seen all this? What must she have thought? But more importantly had she got an eyeful of my...

I couldn't even go there.

I moved so slowly that a snail would've overtaken me on the outside, but I swear the carpet was making a loud noise, or the wall, or maybe it was the vibrations in the air, because my head hurt with the hell of it.

I headed for my kitchen which was left from there. *I think I'm going left; the wall is really fucking loud right now*, as I trailed my fingers along it. Then there were the voices. Not ghostly voices in my head. This was my baseball pro brother arguing with my actress sister.

"—Yeah right," Logan said, and he sounded exhausted.

"You want me to delete the entire freaking Internet?"

"Whatever, JoJo, just don't let him see it."

"It's on TMZ, she's plastered it all over her Instagram, and she tweeted it and the tweet is freaking trending, Lo, there is no way he's not going to see this."

I heard a scuffle. "Give it to me, I'm gonna break the Internet," Logan snapped.

More scuffling, and when I stepped into the kitchen I saw a typical Collins standoff. Logan holding something up high and Josie trying to reach whatever it was, which was my brand new iPad.

"Hey," I croaked, and both of them whirled to face me so fast that Logan threw my iPad, which hit the wall on the other side of the room and smashed in slow motion to the floor. Damn Logan and his freaky throwing arm. I couldn't even be bothered to care; they were there for me, and I was so grateful.

Josie reached me first, guiding me to the kitchen table, a seats-twelve affair made of glass, with chrome legs. It was shit to keep clean, so I never used it. What was the point; it wasn't as if the team was over here having pizza and beers.

I can't even think about beer.

Silently she placed water in my reach, and then a magic plate of pancakes with maple syrup and bananas appeared in front of me. My favorite, and she knew it, although she couldn't cook if it was a matter of life or death, so I knew Logan had made them. I forked up a mouthful, swiping the pancake in the syrup and stabbing at a banana, then chewed and swallowed. I wasn't sure that my taste buds would have survived last night, but after a few bites the banana-pancake-syrup goodness hit me right where I needed it to.

"What did she say?" I asked after I'd finished my first entire pancake. If I knew Logan there would be a whole pile of them somewhere; he stress-cooked, and this right there, his little brother trying to drown his sorrows on the worst day of his life, was definitely going to stress him. Logan didn't understand half the things that had gone wrong for me, and told me so, often, but he had my back the entire way.

"You don't want to know," he said

I looked up at a face so similar to mine, his eyes narrowed, and temper creating twin flags of scarlet on his cheeks.

Josie started, "I'm sorry Tate, but she shared a photo with bed hair in her jammies, pouting—"

Logan cursed, "With a face full of makeup—"

"Logan, shut up. The caption was that she wanted privacy on this *terrible day*, but that she had someone who was helping her find her inner light, or some shit." She air-quoted the last part.

"The usual places picked it up, TMZ ran an article on what happened, blah blah, the ongoing new start."

"What a bitch," Logan snapped, but I placed a hand on his arm.

"No. She's not, Lo. There's something wrong with her, she's so unhappy, and I should never have asked her to marry me. But now, I don't let what she says hurt me."

"She is hurting you, little brother," Josie murmured and patted my cheek.

"I can't think about that, I just want to play hockey."

Logan smacked the counter, making me jump. "I don't get this, Tot. All you need to do is tell people what she was really like, explain that the person you fell in love with changed, and that she blackmailed you into marrying her—"

"She didn't blackmail me. She was honest with me about the despair she felt with life, and I knew I couldn't leave her."

"But if you went out and said something, *anything*, then you wouldn't be seen as the bad guy here."

"I'm not airing… sharing stuff," I managed. The whole mess had been on me too, and I was a god damn gentleman.

"She was the one who went on that reality show and blabbed all your secrets, she's doing this to get sympathy for what was her own freaking fault."

"She has issues," I began, still in defense mode.

"Too right," Logan muttered.

"Look, guys, I don't care anymore, I had my day of self-pity. I'm done with it all now."

"There's something else, and you won't believe it," Logan said

I heard Josie's sharp inhalation, and saw her shake her head in warning. "What?" I was tired of this, I was tired of being the bad guy, the one pushed off the pedestal I didn't even want to be on in the first place. Dallas had wanted a poster boy for manners and friendliness, the league wanted the nice guy they could label a superstar and could wheel out for any and all occasions. They'd made Tate Collins, *superstar*, and all the other parts of me had been destroyed.

What else had been made public? The entire NHL, plus fans, knew I collected *Star Wars* stuff. I'd never made a secret of it, and my first ever Instagram photo was of me in one of the rooms in my Dallas place with whole shelves of merchandise. The fact I was bi, and liked men just as well as women was a secret, but that was my personal life and nothing to do with anyone. I groaned. Fuck. Was it out that I'd had an impossible crush on Tennant Rowe when he was at Dallas, and that I avoided him?

It had to be a *Star Wars* thing. She hated I wasn't into collecting something more, in her words, manly. When I'd pressed her on what she meant by that, all she could come up with was dumbbells.

Who the hell collected dumbbells?

I'd never judged Lacey for what she'd done to my original Boba Fett that first night I'd caught her in bed with another guy. She hadn't seemed herself, and after I'd gently asked the guy to fuck off out of my house, I'd held her for a while as she cried. Then I'd taken a pillow and slept on the couch. Lacey wasn't *the one* but she ticked enough boxes that she could have been.

If I'd tried harder, maybe? I know some of it's on me.

Finding the guy in her bed was bad enough, but having a Boba Fett, with his head snapped off, ripped from his original packaging and thrown at me was more of a shock. That was how numb I'd been to the whole Lacey/Tate love affair.

"She says she might have found new love, and that her heart is finally full blah blah," Josie didn't add anything else, and hell, what about that was going to worry me that it got Logan all riled up?

"I'm pleased for her."

"Tell him about his cat, tell him about Obi" Logan pushed.

Josie held my hand tight, and I knew this was serious.

"What about Obi? What happened?"

"The photo of her in bed? You could see the other guy's arm, but worse than that? He was holding Obi."

You have got to be kidding me.

I HAD THE REST OF THE DAY TO GET MY SHIT TOGETHER, I showered five times, worked out in the huge basement gym for three hours, drank coffee until my hands shook to get some spark in me, mainlined electrolytes, then spent a good four hours out in my huge yard which had a cleared area, with its own net and markings for deck hockey, shooting the puck and not happy until I shot fifty pucks in a row without missing one.

At nine I was in bed. Alone. Logan and Josie had both left after breakfast. Josie back to the set for her vampire time-travel show in LA, and Logan back to San Francisco where he was a starting pitcher.

The only good thing I clung to when I'd been traded to Arizona was that the three of us were close together again. Add Mom and Dad, and I had unconditional love in my corner, and when I pulled into players' parking I had them in my heart, knowing that whatever happened in the Raptors locker room I could get through it.

I was early, hoping to hell I'd be first in, but Ryker was sitting in his cubby, taping up and singing along to whatever was on his iPod. He glanced up when I arrived, and took out the earbuds.

"Hey," he said, and I could tell just from the tone that he'd seen the insta stuff where Lacey had implied shit about me. We'd had an off day; they'd given me a personal day, but now I was back. Tomorrow we were home against

San Diego, a local rivalry, and I had a small hope that today everything would have been forgotten, but no, I could see his expression.

"Hey," I said back, still awkward with Ryker that one day he would find out that his stepdad had been my first crush, but hey, what the hell, life is screwed up.

"Saw all the insta stuff, forget about it," Ryker murmured, and stood to stretch. "No one will mention it, and once we start training—"

A commotion at the door had us both turning. Colorado with one of his famous entrances.

"Sugar, saw the shit on the web, damn dude, it's nice for someone else to take some heat around here."

"Sugar?" I asked, sounded weak, because who the hell knew what was going on in Colorado's head.

"Yeah, Tate-sweet-as-apple-pie, Sugar for short." He tossed me something, and I caught it on reflex. An apple.

"Thanks," I said because I was lost for words, but was pleased he hadn't gone for the whole Tater Tot shit I got from my brother.

Then Colorado moved and behind him stood our captain, Vlad 'The Iceberg' Novikov, all focused as he looked from me to the apple, to Ryker, and to Colorado who was trying for innocent. My heart beat faster, my nerves tingled, and I swear I was getting hard.

What was it about Vlad and the way he came into a room? Or the way he stood? Or talked? Or even freaking breathed.

And why did it get me so flustered?

Chapter Two

Vlad

THERE WAS SOMETHING ABOUT THE CAPTAIN ENTERING THE locker room.

It was similar to when Sister Krygina would walk into the small classroom in our Russian Orthodox school back in Chelyabinsk when my brother Dimi and I were children. She was a thin, dour woman in a black habit and wimple who'd inspired fear and reverence in equal measure. Most of the players quieted, as if I were going to discipline them for joking around. Most. Not all. I did notice the fast look from our newest Raptor, Tate Collins, before he refocused on a shiny red apple. Pity my attention wasn't as easily diverted.

"Yo, Captain Iceberg!" Colorado called out, spinning in an elegant pirouette that made his flowy shirt-robe covering thing flare out around his body. "Check this out."

"It's lovely." I walked around the goalie/rock star/troublemaker. He bounced around in front of me, long, strong legs encased in black leather, sandals on his feet. The man painted his toenails. And sometimes his fingernails. And wore earrings that my mother would've envied.

"Dude, for serious, it's not a lovely look. I mean, lovely?" He smiled a smile that would ensure he never went to bed alone. "Sure, yeah, if I were a chick. No, this is gauzy stage wear that's been adopted for street wear. It's part of the new line I'm designing." He pranced over to Ryker and Tate, looped his arms around their shoulders, and grinned like a monkey high on banana pudding. "Penn Wear, for the rock star in all of us! Like, do you not love that tag line? I made it up. And this is just one of several frocks that I designed to pay reverence to the most amazing sexual deity that ever rocked our tiny world. My idol, Mr. Steven Tyler."

All three fell to their knees to bow and scrape and say they were not worthy. I had no idea what they were giggling about, but seeing Tate smile, even for a few silly moments, did odd things to my stomach. Things that made me feel out of control.

"You have no idea who Steven Tyler is, do you?" Ryker inquired from his position lying on the carpeted floor beside the Raptors logo. One never stepped on or touched the logo itself—that was bad luck—but reclining beside it was acceptable. Americans. No matter how long I lived in this wonderful country I would never fully understand them.

"Of course I do. He's a singer." There. I showed them. "Obviously, a rock and roll singer as only a rock star would cavort around in something that looked like my grandmother's summer robe."

Ryker and Tate howled in laughter. Colorado sniggered, leaped to his feet, and then dashed around the dressing room pretending to be an old Russian woman who played air guitar. Such a jackass. But he did seem to be able to lighten the mood. Alex and Henry walked into the madness, both the young players falling into the lunacy with ease. It was nice actually. The joking and the fun. This team had not always been so friendly. The new regime was working. Slowly. I, for one, was excited for the future.

"Okay children," I shouted after ten or so minutes of banter and roughhousing. "Time for serious business. Today is our first team scrimmage. Coach has assigned us our team roster. You can find your team color listed as soon as I write them down. Suit up in the appropriate color and be on the ice in thirty minutes." I waved a paper filled with Coach's chicken scratching over my head. Striding to the white board that covered one whole wall, I then picked up a red dry erase marker and began copying down the picks. They all gathered around me. I glanced to my right as the fresh smell of citrus danced under my nose. There stood Tate, in hockey pants and socks, his chest and belly bared. He had a tight body, athletic of course, with a light smattering of hair on his chest that narrowed and then dipped into his pants. My eyes flew from that treasure trail back to my job.

Get yourself in hand, Vladislav.

I was the captain. It was my job, my responsibility, to lead the men on and off the ice. Along with other duties the C brought—such as being one of the few men on the ice to speak to and defend my team with the officials and setting the tone for the game—was being "an extra coach" in the locker room as well as on the ice. Being unable to keep my eyes to myself was a sign of weakness. I pushed the tickle of sexual tension down deep and returned to my job.

Tate glanced at me; his deep brown gaze unreadable as the men jostled us around. "I'm playing with you."

"Yes, I know. I'm the one who wrote your name on the board."

A long, long moment passed where we stood there, surrounded by half-naked loud men, him staring up at me as I gazed at him.

"Yo, hey, Sugar and Ice! You two think you can move so I can see where I play?" Colorado shouted, nudging Tate aside with a playful shove. The moment burst into a million bits. I pushed through the men, returning to my cubicle to dress for morning skate.

As soon as I was ready and my stick had been taped properly, I left the madness of the dressing room behind. I needed to clear my head of Tate Collins. The aroma of his shampoo was still haunting me. Thankfully, I bumped into our associate coach outside the skate room. She looked up from the tablet in her hand, a wide smile breaking out upon seeing me.

"Welcome back," Coach Anderson said with a toss of her ponytail over her shoulder.

"It's good to be back. May we talk about alternate captains?"

"Sure. Let's walk and talk. Rowen is watching from

the rafters during this scrimmage. He thinks he's Clint Barton being all *Hawkeye* up there." She gave me a wink and an elbow to the side. I chuckled. We thumped out to the bench area tossing our skate guards to Ross, a new equipment manager. "So, who do you want to suggest for the two alternate captains?"

"It's a hard choice, so many of our players are so young." I stood beside her admiring the tower of pucks piled on the boards. I'd let the men decide who would slap them down. "I'd like to see the alternates have more experience on the ice."

"Yeah, we do have a lot of smooth-cheeked babes," she said, then giggled. "If you're looking for some maturity Tate Collins has been in the pros for a while and has a good reputation, the current fiasco notwithstanding."

"But he is new here. He has not earned a letter in Tucson." I shook my head. "Perhaps in a year or two. The JAR line is impressive, young, but I think Ryker Madsen could handle the A. He's respectful of the officials and maintains a cool head even in heated moments."

"Okay, anyone else?" She tapped on her iPad, then glanced up at me.

"I would like to say Henry but he's not proven himself capable of playing yet, but he does have the personality to handle the responsibility well."

"Agreed. Let's see how he does this season." A few fans filed in behind the glass. Male and female, all with wildly colored hair and holding signs with *COLORADO* surrounded by pink hearts. "Wouldn't the Penn Gang love to see him get a letter?"

"Mm, yes, I'm sure, but thankfully goalies can't leave

the crease so he's stuck there. I'm not sure I'd give him the chance. His temper is like a match-head. One brush and he's on fire." She nodded. We all liked our starting goalie but he was always in trouble. A free spirit our Colorado was. "If I put out my defense partner Eli, would that look as if I were playing favorites?"

"Not at all. Myers has been in the league for several years, is sound and solid, not prone to throwing water bottles at the linesmen."

The men began to file onto the ice. Henry skated over, beamed at us, and cleared the pyramid of pucks to the ice. Eli skated up to me, gave me a poke with a gloved finger, and then raced off with a puck on his stick. That was his not-so-subtle way of informing me it was time to play hockey. Coach Anderson tucked her tablet under her arm.

"Go warm up. We'll work on this later. We still have a week before the finalized roster has to be turned into the league."

I bobbed my head, kicked a puck to my stick, and went for a few laps, shuttling a puck to Eli or taking a soft shot at Colorado in the home crease. The backup tender, Andre, was at the other end of the ice in a white sweater; my half of the team wore brown. Tate Collins exploded into the lazy play of warmups. He streaked past me, a blur of brown, stole my puck, and flew up ice to slam a shot past Andre. All of this took place before I could make the blue line. He circled the net on one skate, left leg up, the celly making him look like a chorus line dancer.

"Pretty boy superstar," Eli muttered at my side, as a whistle blew.

We gathered at center ice, circling our petite associate

coach. I slid in beside Tate, my shoulder bumping his. He threw a sharp glare my way.

"Try to remember that we're on the same team now. Keep the flash and showing off in check." His lips flattened. I moved away to stand with my defensive partner, my gaze and Tate's locked through whatever it was Coach Anderson was telling us. I saw the grit and rebellion in that chocolate-brown gaze of his.

With a smile, we began the scrimmage, white vs brown, and even though I had seen Tate on film, and even played against him once or twice, watching him close-up left me awed, winded, and more than a little aroused. Keeping up with him and Madsen pushed me to my limits. Those ten or so years of age on the young guns showed. They were so fast, so slick, so quick, that it felt as if I no sooner gained the offensive zone to defend when Madsen and Collins would break free. I'd haul my big ass down the ice, then Garcia and Greenaway would steal the puck and race back to my end.

By the end of the practice game my legs were wobbly and it felt like I was skating through tar. I'd be able to soak the aches away in a hot shower and the knowledge that I had managed to pin Alex Garcia to the boards several times despite my advanced age. Water beating down on the back of my neck, eyes closed, I savored the feel of thousands of fingers working my tired muscles.

"Nice play." I knew the voice.

"Thank you," I replied to Tate somewhere to my left. "You also played well."

"You guys have a good solid foundation. Give it another year or two and you'll be contenders."

I flung a look his way, ready to bicker over that year or two comment, and way too late realized how stupid I'd been. The stinging comeback withered when my sight latched onto a wet, naked Tate Collins. He had a body that Adonis would've envied. Thick thighs, a sweet bubble ass, lean waist, wide shoulders. Arms up to douse his armpits, his hair sodden, his ink-worked skin slick, I sucked in a breath and a mouthful of hot water. His dark eyes moved to me. I glanced downward.

"Back in Dallas we used to…"

Whatever he said was a garbled mess. I nodded, made sounds of agreement, and even smiled once when he chuckled at something he'd said. My eyes stayed locked on my feet, the ceiling, the faucets, or the bar of blue, nautical-scented soap in my hand. I lathered at speed, hitting only the high spots as Eli would say, rinsed, said something stupid about a beer sometime, and then left the showers. I pulled on some shorts, a tank top, sneakers with no socks, and got the hell out of the Raptors changing area. Beer. Fuck that. I needed something stronger than beer.

THE SCRIMMAGE HAD KICKED MY ASS, AS HAD THE TIME spent in the showers averting my gaze from Tate's tattooed body. This attraction was growing instead of lessening and I needed to gain some perspective and control. Freewheeling was not my preferred mode of operation. I was happiest when I had things planned out in advance. Spontaneity was not my "happy place" as the Americans are so fond of saying. Feeling the tension tightening my shoulders, I padded to the bar, poured myself two fingers of Stolichnaya, dropped one cube into the vodka, skipped the lemon zest as it was too much work, and went to Frank's massive pen to set him free.

He climbed onto my hand, his claws digging into my wrist as I lifted him out of his cage.

The macaw loved free time, stretching his bright blue wings as he flew around my condo, coming to land on my shoulder as I dropped onto the sofa. I did my best to give him as much time out as I could, along with working on training, as he had an attitude when it came to treats on occasion.

"Alexa, play the *Fearless* album by Taylor Swift," I said while sinking into the sofa cushion. The moment her voice hit the airwaves my tension began to lessen. How was it possible for one woman to be so talented? There was not one album of hers that I didn't have in CD form, vinyl and downloaded for digital play. Taylor was a gift from the gods of music and beauty. If I were straight, or even bisexual like my twin Dimi, I would've married Taylor if she'd have had me.

Women had never appealed to me sexually, unlike my brother. Which made his life in Russia, and his playing in the KHL easier than it had ever been for me. He dated men occasionally but always in secret. At the moment he was seeing a beautiful woman, Lada, who he was madly in love with. He had already bought a ring and had plans to propose next month on their two-year anniversary. Even though I lived and played in America, I still kept a tight rein on my social media presence and the men that I dated. News of my being gay could filter back to Russia where it might make things difficult for my family. So I dated men who understood my need to be discreet and in control of what took place in my bed. So far all had been well, but my tastes had led me to men of an age similar to mine. Not someone younger like Tate Collins, who was *the* face of professional hockey.

"*Vinograd,*" the parrot said, bobbing his red head as his claws sank into my shoulder.

"*Nyet,* I did not get the grapes." I reached up to pet him. He snapped at my hand with a big, black, hooked beak.

"*Mudak! Mudak!*" He squawked, taking to wing to sit atop his crate and glower at me.

"Yes, I'm an asshole," I replied, holding my drink up as a toast to my asshole status before taking a taste. It burned a cold path down to my stomach. My brother had warned me that teaching the bird to cuss in Russian would come back to bite me. He'd been right, damn it. I'd never dreamed my own pet would fling curses at me, and everyone else, who didn't feed him grapes on demand.

My gaze moved from Frank, who was now preening, to the oil on the wall. It was an old thing, a painting of a lady's dressing room or something similar. My great-grandmother had owned it and it had come to us upon her death many years ago. It had hung in our parlor for ages, as my mother fancied it. For some reason when I'd left Russia I'd felt compelled to bring it with me. It did look oddly out of place in my masculine home, but seeing it reminded me of Russia, and my family. Right now, the urge to return home was strong. Putting half a world between myself and my newest teammate would be good. Pity the new season was just about to begin...

Chapter Three

Tate

"I was talking to Henry and he's vanished?"

Thirty minutes to warmups in this our first pre-season game and I needed to find him because I'd already spoken to Sam, my other winger, and when I'd begun chatting to Henry he'd walked off mid-sentence. Chatting to my wingmen was something that worked for me in Dallas, and just a couple of minutes talking casually with your wingmen set the tone for the way the line worked.

Ryker looked up from lacing his skates.

"What did you do or say to him?" he snapped.

"Nothing, I didn't do anything. We were just talking about... never mind what we were talking about." Jeez, why was I on the defensive there? "I was just looking for him."

Ryker went back to lacing but I could see the tension in his shoulders, and then he stalked toward me and inclined his head to indicate that I should follow.

"This is Henry's first full game back on the ice," Ryker said, as soon as we were out of hearing of the rest of the team.

"I know." I'd followed the story that had been Henry's life the last year and had gravitated toward him on my first day with the Raptors. I called him a friend, and I thought Ryker was one as well, but the way he was staring at me, waiting for me to do something he didn't approve of made me feel a hundred kinds of shit.

"Don't mess with his head." He crossed his hands over his chest.

I winced. "I'm not, I wouldn't, I just want to do my usual chat, it's like my... when I was in Dallas—"

"This isn't Dallas," Ryker murmured and drew himself to his full height, and given he was in his skates that made him a little taller than me. I could see his dad in him, that stubborn tilt of his chin, that stony-eyed warning that he would stand his ground, particularly when it concerned his best friend.

"I know it's not Dallas," I said, as patiently as I could. This was better than Dallas, this was a chance for a new start, but I wasn't telling Ryker that.

"If all you're here for is to look fancy ass on the ice and order him around—"

"Now, hang on—"

"He's a good guy—"

"I just want to check in with him, don't you guys check in on each other before games? We did in Dallas—"

"Wassup, Ry, is something wrong with Henry?" Alex came up behind him. Jeez, Alex the back-up was here as well?

What did they think I was going to do with him? Warn him that if he fucked up I'd hire a hitman? Stab him with a skate blade? What?

"He's my wingman, this is just a welfare check." I crossed my arms over my chest, and wondered how it had gone from me and Ryker rolling on the floor laughing at Colorado yesterday to this brick wall today.

"'Just like in Dallas'," Ryker mimicked, and that hurt, because Ryker was one of the good guys, not a man who would lash out at someone and put them down. I could see the temper flash in his eyes and vanish. "I was out of order, sorry," he murmured. "We're just worried about him, is all."

"He had a bad night," Alex murmured.

"You did?" I peered at Ryker, he seemed fine.

Ryker huffed. "Not me, Henry. His partner, Apollo, talked to Adler who told Ten who texted me this morning, to say that Henry wasn't in a good place."

Did I wince when he mentioned Ten's name? Was my unrequited lust for Tennant freaking Rowe written on my face?

Ryker's expression didn't change, so I think I got away with it, and Alex sighed, "I tried to talk to Henry, but he was real quiet, and said he was okay. We just think... look, Coach putting him with you, is it too much?"

"What?" That was what they worried about? "No! I want him on my wing, he's... wait, I don't want to be saying this to you, I want to say this to him. So will you help me and tell me if either of you know where he is?"

Alex and Ryker exchanged looks. I was sure that Henry was hidden away somewhere counting down to the last second he needed to be lined up for hitting the ice in warmups, but I didn't know this arena well enough yet to know where all the best hiding spots were.

"Colorado's rec room," Alex said after a pause.

"Follow the corridor round to the left, take a sharp right, there's a door marked private, he'll be there," Ryker said.

"If Vlad wants to know where we are…" Vlad and his icy Russian-ness sent chills down my spine when he was pissed, but I think it was for all the wrong reasons. And the right ones. I respected him as a captain; he had a control of this team that was beginning to show returns, because it wasn't just power, it was mutual respect and hard work and unfailing encouragement. But, I'd already had my fingers burned with lusting after Ten from afar and see how that had turned out. He'd left Dallas without a backward glance, and we'd never kept in touch even though we'd joined Dallas only a year apart, and were the new kids on the team.

"We'll tell Vlad you're team-building," Alex suggested.

I turned sharply and headed in the direction I'd been told to go, and stopped outside the door marked *Private*. This was not an official private room. I could tell that because it didn't have the fancy sign with the raptor in the corner, instead there was a handwritten piece of paper held up with hockey tape.

Stay the hell out, private space, people might be fucking and it was signed with a big *C*.

Yep, that was Colorado.

He had either had the best idea ever making this room

a private space, or else management just hadn't ventured this far into the bowels of the Raptors' arena and so hadn't found it.

I knocked. Only because the sign made me consider an image in which there was sex going on inside and I didn't want to interrupt anything.

"Henry? It's me," I said, "Tate," I added, because he might not have recognized my voice.

"Come in," Henry called

I cautiously opened the door, found him staring at a wall, in full kit, skate guards on, with his arms over his chest. I closed the door behind me and came to stand by him, noting as I did, the two cozy sofas and the small desk along with a mini coffee maker and a lamp. Someone had gone to great lengths to make this a room a haven for a player to escape to. I followed his gaze to the wall and blinked at the glittery poster that had to be nearly as tall as us, and half as wide.

"Apollo made it," Henry said, and didn't unfold his arms.

It was glittery and pink from corner to corner. Tiny stars formed words, and at the bottom there was a fluffy heart.

Henry cleared his throat and began to read the words on the poster. "I can do this. I am a brilliant hockey player. I can skate. I will score many goals. I can see everything. I am the best." He stopped then.

"I am loved," I continued, and then saw that it was signed in what looked like sparkling gold pen. "And the one who loves you the most is Apollo."

"Why did you want me on your wing?" Henry blurted.

That was an easy one to answer.

"We work so well together, you, me, young Sam." I was only five years older than Sam Bennett, but as a rookie still he would always be young Sam. Until Colorado gave him a nickname and then everything would change.

"What if I can't hear you properly, what if the quieter practices have made it easier to know where you were?"

"You have a preternatural skill at knowing where I am at all times." I pointed at the poster and each item in turn. "You can do this. You are a brilliant hockey player. You can skate, actually faster and better than a hundred players in the NHL. You will score many goals. You can see and hear things that others miss, and you are the best."

"Are you going to tell me that you love me?" He smirked

I returned the smile. "Not today, but I like you dude, so you wanna go warm up and play some hockey?"

He repeated the words once more, and then shook himself loose. "Let's do this."

When we got back to the locker room everyone else had taken places in the line for the ice; only Vlad was left and he looked a combination of pissed and worried. I imagine he was concerned for Henry and angry at me, but I wasn't going to think about his motivations.

"Is Henry okay?" His tone was warm and encouraging, and I could imagine him whispering that in my ear as he.... *Stop now. Remember the Tennant Rowe mess, remember how your stupid crush made you act like a moron.*

Henry nodded. "Yes, Captain."

"Join the line, kid."

Then he turned to me, glanced at me from head to toe and then back to my face. "Shouldn't a phenom like you know that you need skates on the ice?"

Ouch. I could so rise to that, but I didn't. I was never rude to anyone, that was my label, only I could push a little bit, because the way Vlad was staring at me with his gorgeous icy blue eyes, was all kinds of hot.

"Wait?" I said and clutched at my chest. "You're telling me I need skates to play hockey?" I was trying for funny, but maybe I came off as disrespectful. I was just being pure Tate—the smiling sunshine hockey player. But had my shine been dulled by the whole Lacey thing? Was I going to get thrown off the team? Or thumped? Or locked in the sex room for the duration of the game?

Great, I'm second guessing myself.

"Skates on, line up," Vlad snapped at me.

I gave him a salute, laced my skates and headed to my place in the line. Warmup was the team going out before a game and skating around trying to appear cool while loosening muscles, along with as many sexy stretches as we could manage. In warmups I didn't have a lucky place in the line as such, but I ended up with Ryker and Alex, who both gave me looks that asked all the questions about whether Henry was okay. I just nodded as subtly as I could.

We headed onto the ice, and as soon as the brisk air hit me, and my blades touched the cold stuff I was in heaven. The cheering wasn't as loud as it had been at Dallas, but then, this was a pre-season game, and the Raptors weren't known for full arenas at the best of times. I skated a lazy lap of our half of the ice, closing past the San Diego Suns players, who kept throwing me glances. I'd been Tate Collins, first line center for Dallas, with an *A* on my chest, respected, a phenom, even better than the great Tennant Rowe, yet here I was on a team that wasn't likely to break into the top half of the league this year unless there was a miracle. Every time I caught myself in a mirror in the dark red and gold of the Raptors colors it shocked me. Seven years I'd worn green, seven freaking years, and I wondered if I'd ever get used to the colors of fall next to my skin?

We took shots on Colorado, our starting goalie, who for once appeared to be doing what he should have been doing. You know, being the kind of goalie that actually stayed in net and didn't do random cartwheels.

I saw plenty of Colorado fans with boards, a lot for Ryker, even a whole gaggle for Vlad whose head had been photoshopped into a *Top Gun* poster, and two for me.

Two.

When I was used to taking up the entire freaking stadium.

I made a point of heading over to them, one a family with two kids, another two giggling girls.

Welcome to Arizona! The family sign said, and I sent a couple of pucks over the top to the kids.

It's my birthday and all I want is a puck from Tate Collins! This sign was covered in lipstick hearts.

I sent over two pucks, and the girls blew kisses, and I smiled at them politely. Which was the exact opposite to Colorado who was now doing something weird with his stick and sending his fans into a frenzy. I wasn't going to look.

We shuttled pucks between us, worked on some lines, the JAR line up first, Ryker, Jens, and Alex, so in sync it was poetry in motion, and then it was us up next, me, Sam, and Henry. The SHT line?

Yeah, right. I bet we only needed to wait a couple of games before someone on an opposing team made a poster with SHT and added a small 'I' in the middle. We took things slowly, worked our line, got pucks past a posturing Colorado, and caught him on the ass with the last one.

I just wanted him to know we were there.

Then we were off the ice, and I was gratified at least that the arena had filled some more. It could be the draw was seeing Ryker the upcoming bright star of the NHL, or Vlad the icy D-man with his flawless hockey, or maybe it was to support Henry. Hell, but maybe, they were here to see me as well. They might not care about the lies on the television show, or the implication I'd cheated on Lacey, or physically hurt her, maybe they just wanted to watch hockey.

Then I saw the one sign that I wished I hadn't spotted. A huge one of me and Lacey. And a huge jagged line down the middle, and the words were simple. *Tate sucks!*

Great.

We headed to the locker room for the short time before the game, I was between Sam and Henry, and somehow I was deflated, and I couldn't help seeing some of the glances sent my way. No one had come up to me at any point since I arrived in Arizona and asked if what Lacey was saying was true, no one wanted to know specifics why

Dallas had traded me. No one cared enough to ask, but I was sure they were judging me in their silence.

"Guys…" I began, but Ryker stick tapped my leg.

"Fuck that shit, Tate, let's take the Suns down."

The tension was high, but when Colorado began singing 'Don't let the sun go down on me', with accompanying lewd hands movements, everyone laughed.

I hovered near the back of the line. I'd always been one of the first on the ice back at Dallas, but here, I was making a new path for myself, and I didn't believe in the luck thing as much as some of the others here.

"I go last," Vlad said, in that soft accented, yet stern way of his.

"I'll take second last," I suggested, and no one else jumped up and demanded they wanted that space because it was their lucky space. A muscle twitched in Vlad's temple, and I wasn't stupid; I could see he had something to say about that, but the line moved as each player hit the ice and whatever he was going to say was lost in the cheers of the crowd.

Hitting the cold stuff for real was like being home, the speed, the life I felt when I was skating was my happy place. Ryker's line peeled off, along with Vlad and Eli, plus Colorado standing in net, the rest of us headed for the bench and remained standing while Mitzy J, a local mall singer, took us through the national anthem. I bowed my head in respect and my heart swelled as the six thousand or so fans sang along.

In Dallas, I would've been the one out there on the ice for the anthem, first line, standing and representing the team. Here, it was all about me on the benches, waiting for my turn. I was integral to the penalty kill, then I would be playing alongside Ryker, but for now I was waiting with Henry and Sam.

The horn sounded and it was game on.

Ryker was fast, the whole JAR line in sync from the first moment, but the Suns had a D pair all over them, and that was the way it worked. They put the best defense out for the hottest players, but maybe with me in the second line, that would split their D. I was better than Ryker, I knew that, everyone knew that, faster, I could see things that others missed, and maybe that would work in our favor.

I wanted that first line, I wanted an A on my chest, I wanted the Raptors to get to the cup finals, and I was going to help take them there.

I will prove that I'm a good player.

And a good man.

As soon as Henry, Sam and I were over the boards we were hassled and hustled, and I got the sense Henry was nervous, while on the other hand, Sam was like an exuberant puppy. The sync wasn't there yet, but we managed a shot on goal and, but for a slight deflection off a Suns defenseman's stick, that would have been our first goal.

The next time we went over, Henry was all about the confidence, Sam was still a puppy.

In the third and final period with the game tied at two goals each, Henry was on fire, anticipating where I would be, or where Sam was, he was blind passing. I caught the puck, but got blocked in the corner. Sam was there, no longer bouncy, but passionate about getting that disc of rubber on his stick, scrappy and fighting against the opposing team's biggest D-man. As a line we got the puck out of the corner, I threaded the puck through two D-men, passed it to Henry who flew around the back of the net, changing direction on a dime, and shooting past the Suns goalie who'd been fixated on me and Sam. Goal!

When the horn sounded I grabbed at Sam and Henry and we shouted with glee.

This might have been a practice game, we didn't even get points from this for the league stats, but fuck, we were on fire!

The Raptors fans were ecstatic, the Suns fans chanting something I couldn't make out, and we were closing period three with a one goal lead. They called us the Craptors, and we were beating the Suns, a team that had made last year's cup race, even if they did lose in the second round.

Okay, so maybe today they hadn't put out their full roster, not their best like we had, but the pat on the head we got from Coach was the greatest thing ever.

Almost as good as the fist-bump I got from Vlad, and the nod he added in his supremely cool way.

"I got a goal," Henry yelled in my ear.

"You rock!" I shouted back, as the arena erupted into applause.

I looked up. One of the Suns had tripped Vlad, sending him careening into the net, taking it and Colorado on a sliding mess of limbs to the wall. No one was hurt, but this was it, we were on a power play.

Getting the tap to indicate I was going over with Ryker, was like the icing on the freaking cake.

One Ryker-goal later—the puck defying gravity and wobbling on its edge before sliding under the goalie—and there was no chance of the Suns catching up.

This rag-tag Raptors team that worked damn hard to be better?

Yeah. We rocked.

And everything was quiet, and on an even keel.

Until Lacey posted about my attraction to Tennant Rowe, only an hour before I was leaving for a team party.

Fuck. My. Life.

Chapter Four

Vlad

HUMMING TAYLOR'S HIT SONG 'YOU NEED TO CALM Down', I swiped at the steamy mirror above my bathroom sink to make a small hole to see myself. Frank was bathing in the shower now, the stream turned on cool and aimed at the wooden perch made just for my walk-in shower stall.

"Are you enjoying your shower?" I called to the bird in English. He wolf whistled in return. With a smile I ran my hand over my chin, opting out of shaving. Tonight was a party for the team, not a black tie affair. "Are you a handsome bird?" I glanced in the mirror to see him standing with his back to the stream, wings spread wide. "Who is a handsome bird?"

"*Khui!*" Frank cried out, bobbing along the perch joyfully.

I blinked at the profanity. Damn it. I hated it when Dimi was right. "It's not so pleasant to call the man who gives you his shower a dick."

His blue head twisted to the side and he gave me a *click-click* of his tongue. Then he called me a dick again.

I tossed a cuss back at him in Russian, turned off the water, and let him prance and dance on his perch for a moment or two. Giving him my hand, he then climbed on, and I carried him to the bedroom where he sat on a perch by the window to dry and preen as I dressed. I'd just gotten my underwear up over my damp ass when my phone rang.

"Alexa, answer the phone."

"Alexa fuck phone," Frank called and flapped. How grand was it that my parrot was a bilingual curser? The small device sitting beside the TV fed my brother's voice through to me.

"*Privet, brat,*" Dimitri said, his tone light.

"*Privet,*" I replied, opening my closet to look at the vast wardrobe artfully arranged by color. "What are you doing calling me at this time?" I glanced at the alarm clock beside the bed. It was just a few minutes after seven at night. That would put him at two a.m. or so in Russia. "Wait, let me guess. Your girlfriend found out about your ugly feet and kicked you out?"

"Asshole, your feet are just like mine."

I chuckled as I pushed aside some gray slacks. It was a casual affair, according to Henry. His partner Apollo was known for these team parties. They were becoming part of the Raptors experience and popped up with barely any notice. Although this one was to celebrate the end of a rather decent preseason.

"My dick is bigger," I threw over my shoulder as I lifted a silvery type shirt up to inspect it.

"No, mine is. I'm older."

"By seven minutes and that has no bearing on dick size."

"Big dick! Big dick!" Frank squawked.

"I blame that on you," I told Dimi while sliding my arms into my shirt. It would look good with jeans and some casual sandals. Not that I was trying to dress up for my teammates…

"I warned you not to teach him to say bad words. Mama thinks he's possessed by a demon," he said before he sniggered softly. "By the way, Mama and Papa are fine. They were bickering the other day over which of their sons was smartest."

I rolled my eyes. "Surely they chose me."

"Surely not. They said I was smartest, and best-looking. Also, they want you to call them."

"Yes, I will, this Sunday morning as always. Why are you calling?"

"Oh, yes, I forgot you asked. We are planning a party for Mama and Papa's forty-year anniversary. Will you be coming home?"

"Of course, why would you ask me that?" I padded to the dresser to sort through two drawers of folded, ironed blue jeans.

"Because your brain is addled and soft, like your dick."

Frank whistled at the comment. Dimi roared.

I shook my head. "Your brain and my bird's are the same size," I muttered, lifting a new pair of Levi's from the drawer.

"So you say. Good, I'm glad you'll be home. Are you bringing someone?"

That brought me up short. "No, I am…no, there is no one right now."

"I'm sorry for that. Perhaps it's best to not flaunt."

"Yes, perhaps." His comment sounded cruel, and perhaps it was, but it wasn't meant that way. Despite all the hard times we gave each other, Dimi and I were as close as two humans could be. He got hurt and I felt his pain. We had shared the same womb. He spoke only the truth. Flaunting my gayness back home was asking for trouble.

"You know I do want you to be happy," he said, his voice low and soft.

"Yes, I know."

"How you can make someone happy with such a small cock I do not know but…"

"I have a talented mouth," I tossed out.

Dimi choked on a bubble of laughter. We chatted a bit more, about hockey, our teams, and how he was set to be named best goalie of the year if his play continued to be as it had been last season. He thought not, but I was rather sure of his chances.

"Go to bed," I told him. We had always been night people. "Tell Mama I'll call on Sunday. Sleep well. Tell your girl I feel sorry for her putting up with you."

"She loves every moment. Sleep well, brother."

"*Spokoynoy nochi.*"

The call left me smiling, as they always did. Well, not always, but usually. Frank watched me as I stepped into my jeans, zipped them up, and then slid my feet into some leather sandals.

I snapped my fingers and the bird, now partially dry, took wing. He soared through the condo, landing on top of his huge crate. I didn't clip his wings, though many bird owners did. I preferred him to be flighted and took him outside with an aviator harness as often as possible so he could enjoy the outdoors.

"Inside," I said in Russian, holding up my hand. He balked a bit but climbed onto my wrist and let me place him inside his crate. His water and food dishes were full, the crate cleaned of the day's droppings, and there was a new hanging trapeze toy that he grabbed onto and hung upside down from. I closed the door, then locked it with a second small padlock. He knew how to pick the lock that had come with the cage, a lesson I'd learned within the first few days of owning Frank. Coming home to find the bird had shit all over my tidy house and eaten his body weight in bread and nacho corn chips had taught me how incredibly intelligent macaws are. "Be good."

"*Vinograd*?"

"Later." The bird was an empty pit when it came to grapes. I tossed a cover over the crate, gathered up my wallet and keys, and left my home. The desert night was just settling in as I jogged down the stairs to my garage. My condo was one of many new-build townhouses in the Swan Lake Condominium Community located about fifteen minutes outside of Tucson. There were over two hundred units in my gated community, all the same shape and colors—tan and white—and all with two-car garages, small backyards, and central air/heating. There was also a community pool, a homeowners association, and a neighborhood watch. Not that I spent much time swimming or watching the neighborhood. I was either playing hockey during the season or back home in Russia when the season ended. Still, it was a nice home, it was quiet, and no one looked at me in an odd way for being a grumpy Russian who seemed to frighten small children. I jumped into my car, put the roof down, and backed the Audi A7 up.

The ride out to the mountains where Henry and Apollo lived was a lovely one, the sky was purple and pink, the wind was dry and warm, and Taylor was belting out 'Shake it Off' as I pulled up to the Lockhart estate. It was now known as the Desert Lights Halfway House or would be when the renovations were completed in a few months. The sounds of music and laughter rolled around from the back of the mansion, so I followed the noise of a party until I reached the in-ground pool. The big house was cordoned off, signs of construction everywhere, but the pool house where Henry and Apollo lived was wide open.

The pool area was packed with players and their dates/wives/groupies. Colorado was playing croquet while riding on Ryker's back. Oh, perhaps it was polo. Yes, it was polo but with croquet mallets and a rainbow beach ball. How that was working was anyone's guess. Henry was toting Apollo around on his back, and Alex had his boyfriend Sebastian on his bare back. Chuckling at the nonsense, I made my way to the bar outside the brightly lit pool house. Apollo's aunt Sofia was playing barkeep while flirting with one of Colorado's groupies. Our goalie never went anywhere without young men and women in scanty clothes falling all over him. Rock musicians had to have an entourage, or so Penn constantly told us.

Others stood around in small groups, looking at phones, and chatting quietly. I didn't want to know what had caught their attention unless it was a bird video.

"Good evening, Captain!" Sofia said as she gifted me with a smile. "Let me guess, two fingers of vodka with a twist of lemon?"

"Orange twist please," I gave her a wink.

She was a stunning woman, full of life and love. Apollo was lucky to have her in his life. Family was so important. I missed mine terribly. She poured me a drink, then returned to flirting with the groupie. I turned around in time to see Ryker and Colorado tumble into the pool to thunderous applause. An emu wearing a bowler hat ran by with a pulled pork sandwich in its beak. Two girls with big breasts and tiny swimsuits chased the bird, who was named Kricker the Flightless Lord of Ozone. It was Colorado's pet, or so rumor had it, and it travelled around with him like a dog.

I caught movement out of the corner of my eye, and realized Tate was standing there in the shadows. He looked like his world had ended but when he spotted me looking at him the raw pain was replaced by a smile. Shoulders back, he approached me, then stood way too close for my comfort.

"Was that an emu?"

I'd been working hard to keep a safe professional distance from the man until I could strangle the attraction I felt for him. With his bare arm brushing mine and the scent of his citrus shampoo blowing into my face, I realized that

I'd not choked that desire long enough, for it was now pulling in full, hot breaths.

I glanced his way, and then took a second look. He didn't seem like the happy smiling guy that was all we'd seen so far. There was a sadness in his gaze, a wariness, and I think a big helping of awkward temper.

Was that even a thing? *Focus on the Emu question.*

"Yes, his name is Kricker. He's Colorado's, as are the half-naked women and men. I need pulled pork, excuse me." I made a beeline for the food tables, skirting the pool and slipping into the lengthening shadows. The tables looked as if an emu had been helping himself to the food, which he had been. I sighed, took a sip of my drink, and grabbed a handful of chips from a bowl that didn't have feathers in it. When I turned to find who was screaming and why—the emu had stolen a bikini top somehow and its owner was shrieking while pretending to cover her bouncing breasts—I found Tate Collins right in front of me.

This time there was no awkwardness, or any of his shifty-eyed weirdness. No, he was right up in my face and he'd gone straight past wary to angry and incensed. I'd seen this on the ice, when Corey Mason from LA had high-sticked him, but still, this was off-ice when we normally had nice polite Tate and he hadn't sounded pissed when he'd asked about the emu.

"Okay, so, what is it?" he snapped as Kricker made another pass, his big feet slapping on the wet cement, a yellow swimsuit top around his long neck. He'd lost his bowler hat.

"I have no idea what you mean."

"You read the post didn't you! I know everyone else has!"

"I have no idea what you're talking about." I genuinely didn't, but he stormed ahead.

"You think I want to be here tonight? You think that I want to face Ryker after that post?"

"What happened with—?"

"Yet I'm here, facing the laughter, just like I am at every freaking party, just like I am on the ice when I chip in with advice and people look at me like I'm an interloper"

"Tate—"

"But it's you that's worse. Sometimes you won't even look me in the eye. What have I done? What do I need to do? Because it's almost as if you hate me for some reason and I want to know what it is."

"Hate is a strong word that I would not think to—"

"Did you know that I was an alternate captain in Dallas?" His anger shifted and now his voice was low but pumped full of passion. It was an arousing sound, the way he wrapped his words in that subtle Texas twang. It sent blood rushing to my groin. "Hell, another year and they would have given me the C."

"I'm happy for your accomplishments in Dallas, but as I'm sure most of your teammates would like to tell you but are too polite to do so, you are no longer *in* Dallas. You are in Tucson."

His handsome face tightened in anger. "I know where the fuck I am!" He barked, and several heads turned.

I felt the flush of shame creeping up my neck. "Keep your voice down, idiot!" I snarled low in my chest.

He did have the sense to glance around before stalking off, shoulders up, hands in fists. I should have let him go. But no, I had to be a rock-headed Russian with an overinflated value of my importance in other people's lives. I threw back my vodka, placed the empty glass on the table beside an overturned bowl of guacamole, and stormed after Tate. Perhaps it was the moon, full and fat and bright yellow overhead that set me on his trail. Perhaps it was my ego. Lord knows, many lovers had told me I thought highly of myself, which wasn't true, I just knew I had some skills in hockey and lovemaking. Perhaps I felt bad for calling the man an idiot, for he certainly was not a fool.

"I swear to God if you don't back the fuck up…" Tate growled as I rounded a sculpted bush to find him staring at a small koi pond. The sounds of the party had grown distant, just the *thump-thump-thump* of an old Madonna dance song and the occasional womanly squeal.

I could feel his rage and pain from ten feet away. "I need to apologize," I said, taking a small step, the lush grass wetting my toes.

"Fuck you and your apologies," he seethed, his gaze locked on the little cherub peeing into the pond. "I've busted my fucking ass here trying to make the transition smooth, despite all the shit in the press, and all I get from you is flack. You know I would be valuable to this team if you'd just let me."

Shrugging I moved closer. "Tate, I am sorry. My…it's not you, it's me. I've…there are…you'll be a fine alternate captain in a few years. Surely you realize that you must prove yourself a loyal Raptor before we bestow a letter on you?"

I stepped up beside him, watching his emotions dance over his face. He really was incredibly beautiful in the moonlight. I jerked my sight from him, forcing my gaze back to the cement cherub.

"Yeah, I guess I get that, but you're supposed to be above all the petty shit. It doesn't matter what I do in my private life, as long as it doesn't affect my playing, so what is with the attitude from you? Did I piss on your feet in a former life or something?"

"I'm not sure I even believe in reincarnation."

"Dude, it was just a saying. Damn, you Russians are so literal. Like hanging out with Drax."

"I don't know anyone called Drax—"

"From *Guardians of the*— You know what, I'm not even going there."

I needed to get control of this conversation again, because there was definitely something amiss with Tate. "Perhaps we Russians wouldn't need to be so literal if you Americans didn't speak in confusing circles full of double meanings and local flavorings."

That made him glance my way. Which, with the moon captured in his dark eyes and his hair dancing in the dry desert wind, was the tiny spark that would ignite a wildfire. His lips parted. My gaze touched on his mouth, the full lower lip, the divot above his upper lip, and the light scruff he wore so well.

"Zorya has blessed you with the beauty of the evening star." He blinked at me as if I'd just said he were a three-headed, groat-stealing goat. "I…you are not an idiot. I am the idiot."

I reached up to run my fingers along his stubbly jaw. He didn't run or punch me in the throat or kick me in the balls. He stood there with the stars and moon illuminating his face. And I knew that this moment was already terribly out of hand, yet I couldn't stop myself from leaning down a few inches to brush my lips over his.

Chapter Five

Tate

I REARED BACK FROM THE ALMOST-KISS, THE TENDER touch of his lips to mine.

"Fuck you," I snapped, and cast a look around me. Was I being punked?

"No I—"

I turned on my heel and left by the nearest exit, heading down the hill until I came to a seating area with a low wall completely blocked by bushes. I'd just about reached the limit of shit being thrown at me today, and yet I'd still come to this party, just to prove to the team that none of what Lacey said in public was true, or at least that I didn't care what she said.

When she'd signed up for that stupid hockey girlfriends reality show I hadn't even known about it, but at first it had been okay. She's gushed over me as her fiancé, told the world I was the same behind closed doors as I was outside. Respectful, loving, a good friend. Then things began to slip. Rita Dremin, married to the dog-loving Joe from the San Diego Suns, began to tell stories about her husband, and his dogs, and the fact they were trying for a baby, and things shifted. No longer was Lacey the star of the show because she was engaged to *the* Tate Collins, phenom, apple pie guy, because *that* Tate freaking Collins was boring.

So she'd lied, and inside those lies were truths that she'd guessed along the way.

I'd told her that Devin, the C of Dallas, was being hard on us at practice for no reason. In the show she'd made up a story about Devin going nuclear and how everyone was scared of him. She'd even dabbed her eyes for the camera because she was scared for her poor, sweet Tate, pouting that some captains shouldn't be allowed to run their teams by fear.

I'd never said that. I'd never even thought that. But it was the first in so many lies she'd told, that there was no longer any distance between me and the mistruths that people heard. She'd told everyone that I collected *Star Wars* figures, well fuck, is that a crime? Only she told this lie that I'd stolen from a kid at a hospital visit, but she'd told it as a joke, and worst of all she'd implied the kid was dying anyway.

She was a vile human who just wanted the limelight.

Thank god the show had ended, because with things so wrong now at Dallas, I could move on, start again, and show my team that I wasn't what she made me out to be.

Then the worst of it happened—the interviews, the blog posts—and she was riding this fake fame into the sunset. At first it was nothing too bad; she'd implied that I was manipulative, using my money to buy people off. When pressed about the kinds of things I'd allegedly done, she would simply dab her eyes and shake her head. Sometimes she would rub at her side, implying I'd hurt her.

I picked up a stone and threw it into the dark to fuck knows where, then another, and another.

I'd finally thought that somehow I'd made it to a team where I could start again. Here I was just a player, a skater intent on getting his team to the playoffs, I'd even payed Lacey to stop spreading lies.

One million dollars for her silence. Not that it started out as a million for silence, but it sure ended up that way. My heart ached, and I rubbed my chest. For a few brief weeks I'd actually thought that I was... *No. Don't go there.*

I didn't care about the money, I just wanted her to leave me alone, to stop lying, to get over the fact I'd broken off our engagement.

Guilt consumed me and I stopped throwing stones, bending at the waist as the pain in my head grew. I'd really thought I could make a life with Lacey, maybe have some kids, and I'd given her friendship, respect, and fidelity. None of what we'd had was real, just my agent saying my optics were bad, but if I'd said no to start with, if I'd never proposed to her, if...

And now, the worst of what she knew had been added to her blog, that I'd been in lust with freaking Tennant Rowe. Yet I'd still come to this stupid party. I was ashamed, mortified, angry, but I'd showered, shaved, done my hair, dressed nice, and I'd *actually* thought it was a good idea to come here.

Face it, own it, laugh it off.

And then Vlad had joined in the freaking joke, and my heart hurt. I knew the captain found me irritating, probably thought I would break up the Raptors, and from his actions it was clear that beyond the ice he didn't see value in me, but to take what had hit the Internet today and push the joke this far? That was shit, and it hurt, and I needed to work my way through the anger.

"Been looking for you." A voice came from the darkness, and the fury at Vlad subsided in an instant and instead it was embarrassment that flooded me. Ryker had found me.

"You've found me," I didn't move from the bench, but I shuffled to one side in case Ryker wanted to sit down.

"We probably need to talk," Ryker murmured, and sat on the bench at the opposite end.

"Do we have to?" I was mortified that I was stuck in the darkness with the one person I'd hoped to avoid being alone with. In my head I laughed off today's blog post. Ryker would have been in a group of teammates and I would have endured some teasing, but then it would've been over. Planting myself here, all worked up over Vlad had now made me vulnerable to a heartfelt conversation.

"Well, the blog said you were in love with Ten, and that is why he left Dallas, because you made him feel like he didn't fit there."

"I'm sorry, Ryker—"

"Well, it's horseshit. He was traded because of cap space, we all know that. Dallas couldn't have both of you. So anyway, the Railers is the best thing that ever happened to him, and he *didn't* leave Dallas because of you."

What was Ryker saying? He didn't sound like he was accusing me, if anything he sounded like he was supporting me.

"None of it was true."

"Ten always thought you were a better player."

"He did?"

"Yeah, felt like he would always be second best, and that he'd find first line success elsewhere. Not only did he find that with the Railers, but he found Dad."

I buried my face in my hands. Ryker was warning me off from his stepdad. I knew this was going to happen. Fucking Lacey and her fucking blog post.

"I'm sorry Ry, you know I wouldn't—"

"I had this huge poster on my wall, of you and Ten, remember that back-to-back photo shoot you did for Bauer?" He didn't wait for an answer, "Two really gorgeous guys, and I slashed you so hard."

"'Slashed'?"

"You and Ten, kissing and all kinds of romantic storylines in my head, it's what teenagers do, you know; you can't tell anyone though, because now you know an embarrassing story about me, and we're even."

It took me a moment to process. "You're not angry about what was posted?"

"That you had a thing for my stepdad? You're a red-blooded bisexual male, you'd be an idiot not to. Well, at least, I assume you're bi, given the whole nearly married thing, unless that was—"

"Bi, yes, but I promise you it was a crush on him, and I'd never act on what I used to feel about Ten—"

"You mean try and get between Dad and him?" Ryker

huffed and then sidled closer and elbowed me in the side. "Dude, you'd be on the losing side there; besides, my old man still has some moves."

I wanted to confide in Ryker, thought maybe I had a friend here, I wanted to tell him how Vlad had pretend-kissed me, and that he'd made me feel like shit, but I didn't. I'd shared things like that before, with Lacey, and look where that had gotten me.

"So, are there any other secrets your ex is going to reveal?"

I couldn't think of any truths that she could pass around like candy, hoping to win friends and influence people. I thought the Ten thing was probably the worst of it. Oh wait, there was one more thing.

"I cried at the end of *Titanic,* and *A Dog's Life*," I admitted, "and that is not what big, strong, physical hockey players do."

Ryker pulled out his phone, and in a few keystrokes he'd done something on Instagram, and my phone vibrated, because, of course I followed the guys on the team who had social media accounts. Ryker's was one of the most vocal, for LGBTQ+ inclusion, for pranks, for puppies, kittens, kids in need. He posted nearly every day with one thing or another, and a lot of times it was of him and his gorgeous Jacob.

"Look at your phone," Ryker instructed.

I pulled out my phone, clicking the notification that he'd posted, and I couldn't help a snort of laughter. I read out his post, "Is it just me who cries at the end of *Titanic* and *A Dog's Life*? Asking for a Friend." Then there were the additional yes and no options, and even in the few seconds it had been live there had been votes.

"Get out ahead of it, see?" Ryker murmured. "Anyway, we need your help dude, Apollo is threatening to serve up emu steak on the barbecue, wanna go see?"

As long as I don't have to talk to Vlad. "I'll be right up." Then, as soon as Ryker had fist-bumped me and left, I pressed the No button on the Instagram question, and in doing so I owned the fact that I cried as well, and it wasn't a secret anymore.

I still had to face the Railers, I still had to play Tennant Rowe and be able to look him in the eye and own that as well, but hell, I was a grown-ass man, and I could do that in a heartbeat.

So I headed back and entered into the jokey debate about how great emu steak would be, particularly with proper Texas barbecue sauce, and it only ended when Colorado sat on Alex's head.

Vlad was nowhere to be seen, and a small part of me was concerned. Of course largely, I remained angry that he'd decided to join in on the pranking in such an intimate way, kissing me for God's sake, still, where was he? Maybe he hadn't been pranking me, maybe he had, but I didn't want to get off on the wrong foot with him, so armed with two plates of food, I headed for the last place I'd seen him, and found him with ease. He was sitting on the grass by the water, in a lotus position, and for a second I wondered if I was interrupting some weird-ass middle-of-a-party yoga session. Then the anger thing pushed to the front and I whistled, a little pleased when he jumped and unfolded himself. I thrust the plate of food at him as he stood. He fumbled, then caught it, before placing it with care on the ground

"I apologize," he ground out, "it was inappropriate—"

"Just because I had a thing for Tennant Rowe doesn't mean that anyone can just—"

"You have a thing for Rowe?"

"Had. I *had* a thing—"

"Oh." He looked lost for words, even a little disappointed.

I put my food down next to his. "Wait, you mean you actually hadn't read today's blog post from my former fiancée?"

"No. I mean, I read a nature article about global warming and birds that—"

"Then you had *no* idea I had a thing for Tennant Rowe?"

"I don't understand this *thing* you keep saying, were you in a relationship with—?"

"God, no."

If it was possible, he seemed even more confused, and I found I was liking his confidence slipping. This was a tiny glimpse of the man beneath the icy façade.

"So…" he began, "the apology."

"Why did you kiss me?"

"Tate—"

"Is this some Russian anti-gay thing where you trick people out of the closet, and then give them hell?"

He reared back at that, and the shock on his face was real. "No—"

"Then who the hell is Zorya and why does she think I deserve to be a star?"

He gaped, then stepped away from me, and I genuinely thought he was making a run for it, but I needed an answer and so I followed him. All too soon I realized my error as we were now farther back in darkness, isolated from the rest of the team, and he had his back to a palm tree. Not only that, but there was only a foot between us.

"Vlad, who is Zorya?" I asked again, "sister, mom, friend… girlfriend?"

He cleared his throat, "Zorya is the Goddess of the Dawn and the daughter of the sun god Dazbog. It's a… thing."

Gods and goddesses? Who would have thought that our focused, stubborn, icy captain had the heart of a poet. Good to know. Also, his gruff Russian accent was hella sexy and I had him backed up against a tree. For some reason he thought this goddess had blessed me with something cool like being a star. So what the hell had he kissed me for? Was it even possible that my lust toward him was reciprocated? Was it feasible that all the time spent pining for Ten could be forgotten and I'd actually get a proper kiss from Vlad?

"If you weren't messing with me before, then how about kissing me again?" I fronted, chest out, shoulders back.

"It's a bad idea," he said, and attempted to sidestep me. He was a defender, he was bigger than me, he could've hip checked me out of the way and I'd have been toast, but I was younger, and faster. I blocked him in an instant, and hoped he wasn't stupid enough to shove one of his best players into the undergrowth.

He stepped left, I followed him, and he growled at me, "*eto glupo nepravil'no.*"

"What does that mean?"

He muttered it again, then sighed. "That this is stupid wrong," he explained.

He feinted right, then left, but I knew his moves; I'd watched him on the ice, gone up against him often enough in the last seven years, seen the intentions in his posture, knew him so well, and abruptly we were face-to-face and there was nothing between us at all.

With a growl he grasped my arms, lifted me off the ground and turned us so that I was the one with my back to the tree. I was hard already, I mean, fuck, he'd just lifted me, and turned me and—

The kiss was brutal at first, clashing teeth, and parrying tongues, and it was heat and fire, and lust, and everything that made me hard. He cursed between kisses, pressing me against the tree, and I cursed back, at least in my head. I scrambled to get a hold of him, gripping his shirt, his arms, holding on for dear life.

Then the kisses slowed, and he cradled my face, "*eto glupo nepravil'no,*" he repeated

I slid my hand from his hip, up his chest, and to his face, and I had all the words inside me that I wanted to say.

"Captain!" Colorado called from somewhere close. "Yo, Iceman, we have a barbecue sauce emu emergency!"

We parted so fast that Vlad stumbled and I reached out to steady him, only for him to turn his back on me and stride away. So much for a connection.

I stayed where I was for a good five minutes, or at least

until my cock had decided it was getting nothing, and went back to sleep, then sauntered up to join the rest of the guys.

"Sugar!" Colorado yelled, and everyone turned to look at me. "Iceman was no help at all, you tell these assholes that emu steak is not on the menu!" He had laughter in his eyes, he knew it was all a joke, and I knew he loved an ongoing joke.

"I'd like to see one of you catch it first," I deadpanned, and various guys started bragging how the emu didn't stand a chance against them. Particularly if said emu was on skates and therefore at a disadvantage. There was laughter, and Vlad was right in the middle of it, even if he did glance at me every so often as if I was a question that needed an answer. I was done with tonight, and I genuinely hoped that the drama was over. I was so close to giving my excuses to leave but Colorado wasn't letting me get away with things so easy.

"So, Sugar, is it true what I read about you and Tennant Rowe?"

I fake-clutched my chest. "I didn't even know you could read, Colorado."

He snorted, and then made a lewd action with his hands, "were you bumping uglies?" Colorado smirked at me.

Alex smacked him upside the head, Ryker shoved him, and not a single guy was staring at me with anything like distaste or hate. In fact everyone was laughing; even Vlad had a cautious smile.

"I wish," I deadpanned, and Ryker snorted a laugh and slapped me on the back.

Maybe I wasn't tired after all, in fact I thought I'd stay

there, join in the crap, stare a bit at Vlad when he wasn't looking, and chill.

Perfect.

Well, perfect, if only I hadn't spotted Vlad staring at me with utter focus on several occasions.

Damn the man for being sex on legs, with his intriguing eyes, and his tight ass, and his muscles, and damn my weakness for all of those things.

Chapter Six

Vlad

WEEKS SINCE THAT KISS, AND I CLUNG HARD TO A SAYING my father had that goes something like, "If you work hard enough all your troubles will disappear."

My father, as much as I loved him, was wrong about that. I had been working harder than ever for over thirty days, and the biggest trouble that I had was still showering naked. Of course I did not expect Tate to bathe fully clothed; that would have been foolish. But he could have been less attractive. His ass could've been flabby, his cock tiny, his smile lacking teeth. Many players lacked teeth. Why wasn't he also? And why was I mulling over his smile, ass, and prick while clocking in a few miles on the stationary bike. I needed to pedal harder. Sweat ran into my eyes, my thighs screamed, but I cranked up my speed and incline.

"You know if that bike ever breaks free your pale ass will be in Mammoth before you can stop."

I threw a dark look at Colorado lounging against the wall of the training room sipping some sort of dark red guava drink. He was clad only in shorts and flip-flops with big purple rubber flowers. And of course tattoos. Most were flaming skulls or flaming guitars or flaming pigs. His newest was on his pectoral and it was of that stupid emu complete with bowler hat.

"My pale ass will be fine." I slowed nominally but left the incline steep. He made a sound around his straw, tossed his long dark hair from his face, and continued to stand there watching. After another half mile I had to ask. "Is there something that you wish from me?"

"Yeah, well, sort of." He flip-flopped over and climbed onto the empty bicycle beside me. My eyes rolled. This was not what I wanted this morning. Did he not realize that I had to purge my body and mind before the rest of the team showed up? "Man, I hate bikes. They squish my balls."

I plucked the towel draped over the handlebars to mop my face. "Then perhaps you should go find something else to do. The elliptical way over there?" I jerked my sodden head toward the far side of the room.

"Nah, this is good. I'll just shift the boys to the right." Which he did with his free hand. "So, about you and Tate…"

My foot slid off the pedal. I tossed another glare his way. He waggled one dark eyebrow while innocently sucking on a yellow straw.

"Do not be an idiot. There is nothing between Tate and me."

"Right, because you're straight and he's not this fucking sexy-ass beast. Come on, Iceman, bark up the tea."

I blinked at his confusing words and because the salt of my sweat was burning my eyes. "I don't drink tea."

"No, you asshole. Give me the tea. Like, in gossip, you know what gossip is, right?" He made a rude noise with his straw, a slurpy sound that grated on my already frayed nerves.

"Of course I know what gossip is. I've lived and played in this country for over thirteen years. My grasp of your chaotic language is probably better than yours."

"You didn't know what bark up the tea meant, just saying." He shrugged, slurped, and then settled his gaze on me. "Anyway, so you and Tate have a vibe thing. I've seen it since the end of the preseason party a month ago."

I stopped pedaling completely. "You've seen nothing. There is nothing to see. He is my teammate. I'm his captain. Having a thing with him would be unprofessional."

"Dude, seriously? Unprofessional?"

"Yes, unprofessional. People would say he had an unfair advantage, that I was coddling him, giving him preferential treatment. Also, I am not gay."

"Oh, so it's that way, then? Are you hiding it because you're Russian? I mean, I get that if you are. Got to think of the folks back home and all…"

"No, it is not because I'm Russian. I…there is nothing to hide because I am not… Why are you looking at me in that manner?" I slid off the bike, legs wobbly, and stumbled for the door.

"Hey, Icey Cool, come on, don't give me the cold shoulder." He howled at his comment. I growled. Penn appeared beside me, grinning like a drunken dodo. "Dude, Ice, Cap, come on. Seriously, I'm just trying to get you to see what we *all* see."

I spun on our goalie, hands itching to shove him into the nearest wall and knock some sense into his head. "You have fed too much on the tit of rock and roll!"

"Oh my God, that is such a cool song title. Suckled on the tit of rock and roll! Dude! You're a fucking genius!" He flung his drink over his shoulder, grabbed my face with both hands, and kissed me on the mouth.

I sputtered and scrubbed the guava taste from my lips. Penn raced out of the room yelling that he needed a piano stat. I glanced around to see Alex, Ryker, Henry, and of course Tate standing in the doorway mouths agape.

"I did not... he kissed me for...a song title. I'm not gay."

Four heads bobbed slowly.

"Totes."

"Right."

"Never thought otherwise."

Tate said nothing, then walked off with his spine stiff.

I threw a string of Russian curses at the young players gawking at me, then set off after Tate. Damn that fucking Colorado Penn and his loose lips. I jogged to catch up with the leaner, faster, and younger man. He jerked to a halt when I touched his shoulder. I moved around him, face-to-face, to block his path to the dressing room.

"I do not go around kissing men as a habit," I told him, my voice low and aiming for secretive.

"You kissed me, but hey, that was a month ago and then when I kissed you it was all Fuck off, Tate! So I fucked off."

"I never told you to fuck off. I just..." I threw a look up and down the corridor. There were far too many people here. "This is not the place for this. Come to my home. For a dinner. We will talk."

He bristled a bit. "You're my captain on the ice but not off. If you want me to come over, ask nicely like a friend who's had his tongue in my mouth a few times."

This man. There wasn't one button I owned that he did not push, repeatedly, every damn day. Being in such a close proximity with him was stripping my senses.

"Fine," I pushed through clenched teeth. "Will you come over for my place to dinner? For dinner. To my place. Fuck you."

The bastard had the gall to smile, just a bit. "I'll be there at seven. Fuck you." And off he went, skirting around me, heading back to join up with his friends. Sweaty towel in hand I stood there in the hall looking like a complete jackass.

"*Bolvan,*" I muttered, calling myself a jackass in two tongues to drive home the point.

Eli lobbed a stinking sock at my head. That broke the spell for Tate, his smile, and his ass in those shorts. We would talk tonight. All would be settled and my life could return to where it had been before Tate Collins had blown into it like a typhoon.

· · ·

MY FIRST MISTAKE, WHICH WAS ONE OF MANY I'D MADE over the past two months, was to be stupid enough to think that Tate being in my home would somehow squash the attraction we had for each other. He fit into my condo well, looked far too good walking through my living room, his dark eyes rounding when he spied Frank.

"Does he talk?" Tate asked as he approached the huge cage in the corner. His jeans and tank top were nicely cut, baring his arms and most of his shoulders and neck. I loved a long neck on a man.

"*Ublyudok!*" Frank yelled, clicking his beak at this stranger staring at him.

Tate's bright brown gaze swiveled from the macaw to me. "How cool! He speaks Russian. What did he just say? Hello or something?"

"Motherfucker," I replied. Tate laughed aloud. A sound that felt warm and nice in my usually quiet condo. "Please do not stick your finger into the cage. He bites. It is a problem from his previous owner and I have not fixed it yet. We are working on it."

"Got it." He shoved his hands into his front pockets, but still stood there admiring the bird.

The timer in the kitchen went off.

"I must take out our dinner. Please, sit and be comfortable. Is a glass of white wine to your liking?"

"I'll just have a beer, or...no, uhm, just some water with lemon."

"Yes, of course. Sit."

I scurried off into the kitchen to remove the garlic potatoes and chicken one-dish meal I had prepared. With a big salad, this was a perfect dinner for two athletes sitting down to talk. I placed the chicken on a trivet, moving around my kitchen to the fridge where I had the salad stored.

"So, you like Taylor Swift?" I glanced up from the inside of my refrigerator to see Tate now in the kitchen. Did he never listen to directions? "You own every CD she ever made? Or did you miss her kindergarten Christmas concert?"

"Snooping is unbecoming," I mumbled as I pulled the big bowl of salad from the fridge. He chuckled. "My love for Taylor is a private matter."

"Yeah well if you're trying to hide something maybe you shouldn't be so obvious."

I knew that he meant that in reference to all the CDs and vinyl albums lined up on one long shelf on my bookcase. Or at least I thought he meant it in that manner. Hands filled with a cold glass bowl heaped with romaine, iceberg, radish slices, carrots, and tiny bits of black olive, I stared at him openly, unable to form a sensible reply. Which was my standard operating procedure with Tate nearby.

"He kissed me," I said for some bizarre reason. It was important that he know that I hadn't initiated anything like I had with us. "For a song about tits." He arched any eyebrow. "It was...you should have been there to understand it best. You...this thing with us, this attraction...it's making me off-center. Wobbly. I think perhaps we should not act on our lusts anymore until after the season is over."

"Uh-huh. Is that what you really want?" He walked over, took the salad, placed it on the island, and then planted himself right in front of me. "I'm not going to pressure you. I have enough shit to deal with, let alone adding dating my team captain to the list."

His eyes were lovely. Thick sweeping lashes and eyes that were brown with flecks of gold, like those little Russian chocolate caramel candies everyone always wanted me to bring back to the states.

"You should be in the living room."

"Hard to eat in the living room when the food is out here."

"I have meat."

"Yeah, I've noticed."

I lunged for him at the same time he moved toward me. I captured his head in my hands, slanted my mouth over his, and dove into his mouth like a man starved. Truly, I had been. It had been five weeks or so since we'd kissed at the party. A lifetime, to be sure. He gripped my hips, tugging madly to get our cocks aligned. When they brushed, he gasped. I inhaled his breath, savored it, and then moved from his lips to his neck. A throaty moan bubbled out of him. I rolled his head this way and that, lapping over his Adam's apple, his new whiskers rough on my tongue. I nibbled an ear, tugged on the lobe, and felt him melting into my arms.

"Fuck yes," he panted when I caught his hands and lifted them above his head. Then he was pinned to the inside of the refrigerator, the cold air on his back, his head on the freezer, which was still shut. I licked into his mouth again, demanding a hotter response, which he gave me.

"Stay like this, arms up, do not move," I huffed beside his ear. He grunted, rotating his pelvis against mine. I was already close so I moved away, dropping to my knees to free the cock that I'd fantasized about tasting for what seemed like years.

"Fuck, oh fuck yeah," Tate panted when I took him in hand and licked at the slit of his prick. A droplet of pre-cum appeared. I licked it off, ran my fingernail over the underside of his dick, smiling wide when he whimpered my name. "Shit I…" I heard his fingers scrabbling over the top of the fridge as he worked to stay where I had put him. "Fuck, just…ah shit."

"You're mine now, sweet one."

"Say that in Russian. Call me sugar in Russian."

I lapped at his cockhead, watching his face as passion overwhelmed him. God yes, he was beautiful and he was mine. Perhaps just for this half hour or maybe for a night, for this was perhaps the most unprofessional thing I had ever done.

I whispered what he wanted to hear right before I swallowed his thick cock to the root. He cried out. Frank replied with a scathing curse word that Tate wouldn't have understood, thank God. The man unraveled. He was vocal, yet obedient. Thrusting his hips to pump his cock in and out of my mouth while gripping the freezer door for dear life, he fucked my mouth wantonly. I egged him on, sucking harder when he did something that I liked, easing off when he didn't. The first spurt of cum that hit my tongue made my balls contract but I tamped it down. I wanted him to get me off, one-handed, right there in the kitchen.

His taste filled my mouth. I swallowed each pulse, then got to my feet. His eyes were black with lust. I covered his mouth with mine, smearing his taste over his tongue. He bucked for a moment longer, lost in the final tremors of his orgasm. Then with a gasping breath I took one hand down and pressed it against my crotch.

"Use your hand," I said over his kiss-swollen lips. He nodded, his gaze fuzzy and sensual. I kissed him again and again. He freed my cock. I bit down on his lower lip, gently, and he moaned. Arching into his palm when his hand circled me, he tugged with jerky motions, his fingers toying with my foreskin as if it were a novelty. "Have you never been with a man who was uncircumcised?"

"I… no…not just…uhm, there were a few guys in college, hand jobs, all cut. I…fuck that is sexy."

"You are sexy. Too sexy for my mind."

"Too sexy for your shirt too?" he asked with a soft laugh.

"Your shirt *is* sexy."

"Oh my God, Drax, just stop being so you."

His palm rolled over the head of my dick and I lost my train of thought. For a man with little experience with other men he was certainly working me with skill. Or perhaps it was just that it was Tate writhing in my arms, jerking me off, wearing the love bites I'd put on him. Seeing those dark marks, I lowered my head to give him one more as he worked me into a frenzy. When I came my teeth sank into his neck. He worked my spunk all over me, whispering for me to suck harder, mark him. So I did; I sucked harder. When I could breathe properly, I moved from his mottled neck back to his mouth. Our kisses were softer now that the fire had burned down a bit.

"This is not how this was to go," I confessed, nibbling at the corner of his mouth.

"Yeah, I figured." He pulled his hand out of my pants. I groaned at the loss. Then he rose a bit to capture my mouth. "My ass is cold but I don't want to stop kissing you."

"Yes, I..." I stepped back, disliking the cool air blowing between us. "Me either, but..." I looked at him, his flushed face, his brown eyes heavy with satisfaction and warmth, his arm still obediently over his head, his clothes rucked up and sideways, and knew then that I'd never be able to go back to just being his teammate. "Yes, we should...you should wash your hands."

"Tell me to move," he whispered. "Give me permission."

Oh. Fuck. He'd found me out all too fast.

"Go wash up, then we will talk." I ran my thumb along his lower lip and felt him tremble. I stole one final kiss before moving away to give him room to right himself. I tucked and zipped, my eyes never leaving Tate's while he did the same.

"Bathroom?" he asked, his voice soft and appealing. How had he read me so quickly? And why was I now unable to picture a tomorrow that wasn't wrapped up in the taste of him on my tongue and the subtle dip of his head as we played with this new dynamic.

"By the front door is a powder room. Go wash up." I pushed the door of the fridge shut. Color lit his cheeks. "Come back and we'll eat and talk." He nodded, and he seemed unable or unsure of what to say or how. I gave him a smile. "Go, clean up. We'll work this all out somehow. Go now, Tate."

He shuffled off, his gait a little off-kilter. Which exactly how my thoughts, hell, my whole world, now were.

Chapter Seven

Tate

THE POWDER ROOM HAD A MIRROR OVER THE BASIN, AND as I washed my hands I stared at my reflection and wondered why I didn't appear to be any different. Surely what I'd just done, the connection, the lust, would have made me change outwardly. I could see the signs of Vlad's touch on me, dark bruises near my throat, my hair sticking up this way and that, and my skin reddened from stubble, but it wasn't in the way I looked that made me feel as if my world had been rocked.

I still felt unsteady on my feet.

The way he'd told me to leave my hands where they were, the hardness of the refrigerator behind me, Vlad on his knees sucking me down, then the heat of him spilling over my hand. It was sensory overload, and I gripped the basin. I'd never experienced an orgasm that intense, had never been spoken to in that way.

Perfect Tate Collins with his manners, and his clean cut

All-American looks, squeaky clean, nice to everyone? That wasn't who I felt inside right now. Inside, I was lust and need and raw with emotions.

"You okay?" Vlad asked softly from outside the door. I don't even know how long I'd been staring at myself checking for differences, but the water was still running and the mirror was fogging up. It was as if the old Tate was being misted over, and maybe this new Tate, the one tarnished by Lacey and her shit was now free to do what he wanted. He could still be the guy he was inside, caring, a good friend, polite to everyone, working for charity, playing good hockey, but maybe he could allow this other side of him free now.

If Vlad even wanted to do this again.

"Tate?" Vlad murmured, and I heard a noise, like maybe he was resting his forehead on the door. I was fucking this up staying in here like a coward, when I wanted to be *out there* with Vlad, getting to know him better, kissing, maybe taking it further, maybe...

Stop thinking and get the hell out of the bathroom.

I opened the door, cautiously, in case Vlad was leaning on it, but he'd moved away and was leaning on the wall opposite.

"I can take you home," he said, his hands in his pockets, not moving an inch, and I saw in an instant what my messing around in the bathroom had caused. Doubt. So much doubt. He probably thought I regretted what we'd done.

"No, I—"

"As your captain I can tell you what to do on the ice, but in here, when it's us, I would ask that you don't tell people about me... I have family to consider, and I know you're a good man, but—"

I launched myself at him, cut off his words with a messy, uncoordinated kiss, and nearly climbed him like a freaking tree. He grabbed me and held me steady as we slid down the wall and I straddled his lap. He was in shock, his eyes wide, and we stared at each other for the longest time.

"I would never tell anyone—"

"I'm sorry if I—"

We talked over each other, and with my polite gene I smiled, "You first."

"I'm sorry if I implied you would ever—"

I kissed him again. "No apologies, but you maybe want to take this into the bedroom?"

He levered me off him, catching me before I fell, and then he tugged me down past the kitchen.

We were so close to getting inside and for me to experience everything I'd dreamed about when his cell made this obnoxious alarm noise and he stopped.

"Colorado *Ublyudok!*"

Frank copied him immediately. Although why Colorado's name was in there, I didn't know.

He released his hold on me and picked up the cell, connecting the call and letting off a stream of obscenities that were a mix of Russian and American. I heard someone shouting back.

"What!" He was incredulous. "No, I'm not— *Ublyudok!* Thirty minutes and don't you fucking leave, you moronic asshole *kusok der'ma.*"

He slammed the phone onto the counter, bent his head,

and I could see the tension in every corded muscle of him, his hands curling into fists as if he wanted to hit someone so hard they'd end up through the Plexiglass at the arena. His reaction didn't scare me since he was all about control, but every so often, where the Raptors were concerned there were glimpses of an awesome Russian temper. This was different, though.

"What's happened?" I asked, and took a step closer to him, wondering if we were in a place where I could touch his arm to calm him down.

"You don't want to know," he ground out, "Fucking Colorado! He'll be the death of me."

We all knew Colorado was a live-wire, or a loose cannon, or any combination of words that described someone with tentative control on himself, but I wasn't sure I'd ever seen Vlad curse as much as this before. He was the captain who dealt with officials in a calm, professional manner, the one who had every team member's back, but whatever Colorado had done now was clearly a long way past bad.

"What did he do?"

He left out a sigh, then turned to face me. "He's holed up in his house with that fucking emu, and is refusing to come out."

"How do you know that? Why did he call you?"

"Because Animal Control is outside his place, he's broken a hundred rules, and now they're calling in the cops, and he calls me every single goddamn time he messes up. So often I even have a ringtone just for him."

"I'll come with you."

Temper flared in his eyes. "How will that look? You

want Colorado seeing us together, with my mark on your neck?"

I instinctively covered the place I'd seen the bruise, and the temper left him as soon as it had appeared. He pulled me into his arms and held me close.

"I'm sorry, *dorogoy*."

"What does that mean?"

He looked past me at the door. "I have to deal with this, call management, make this less than it is before he destroys everything."

"I understand."

"You should go home."

"I can stay here." *Wait for you to come back.*

"Go home, we have the flight to Calgary tomorrow," he said, and I imagine he was trying for reassuring, but his head was elsewhere. He was using his captain voice, and I didn't argue. Then he cradled my face and kissed me gently. "I'm sorry, *dorogoy*. So sorry."

WHEN I GOT HOME I WAS AT A LOSS OF WHAT TO DO IN THE huge space, I showered, made an omelet after my stomach reminded me I'd had nothing to eat, and then it was an aimless wander through empty rooms. Property was cheaper in Tucson than it had been in Dallas, but then I'd bought an apartment in downtown Dallas close to the Arts District as an investment and it was sure as shit expensive there. This place was rented, I didn't own one small part of it, and it was too big for me. I wanted something more like Vlad's, open plan with a view, a kitchen where you could prepare food and have friends propped up against the counter. Renting was a waste, but I had all this money just sitting there, investments that I had control over, some property, some more speculative and I earned more than Vlad did, more than anyone on the Raptors. They'd paid a huge price to have me come here, and I guess our first away game would show them if I was worth it. Only, we were up against a Calgary team that was still hot from last year's cup run.

From there it was onto Vancouver, then all the way back to Toronto. Eight days away from Tucson, the Canadian road trip early in the season was going to be a wakeup call for the team.

I packed my bag efficiently, left it by the door, rolled my shoulders, then took my phone to bed with me. It was cold comfort, considering I could have been having sex with a hot Russian, but I scanned Twitter and it wasn't long before I found my first mention of Colorado.

"Hockey Player Holds Exotic Pet Emu Hostage," I read out loud, and followed links to discover that Animal Control, backed up by Tucson's finest, had liberated the emu from a very sad-looking Colorado. The way the scene was lit it was obvious that there were arc lights from above, possibly a helicopter? As the emu was led from the scene, I switched to the local television channel.

Colorado was on his doorstep, remonstrating at length with a cop, and then I saw Vlad, well, I saw his hand, as Colorado was yanked back into his house. Cops went in as well, and the feed ended, although both Colorado and Kricker were trending on Twitter when I went to sleep.

It remained in the news the next morning. Lots of codes were mentioned regarding prohibited wild animals, and it didn't seem to matter that Colorado's claim that he'd rescued the bird from a drug dealer sounded reasonable. Mainly because the words drug dealer were anywhere near his name or the team, and also that with his long hair and tattoos and his rangy body he could pass for a bad guy in a cop procedural. They interviewed management on breakfast news, and then Vlad, and he was stony-faced, but reassuring, firm, but sincere, as he explained it was all nothing and just a huge misunderstanding.

By the time I was ready to leave for the small private airport we flew from, the whole event had become a joke, with ten new memes in the past hour. Only I didn't think it *really* was over, because when I arrived at Flying Diamond Airport, Colorado was nowhere to be seen, and our backup goalie, Andre, was onboard with everyone huddled around him, chatting about the incident.

"He's off the team for sure."

"Tell me again about the naked bit—"

"Was the emu naked?"

"Not the emu, idiot, all emus are naked, I mean the girls—"

"I bet management is pissed—"

"If we lose him though—"

"How did he not know that—?"

Everyone fell silent and I glanced over my shoulder to see Vlad had arrived and behind him was a contrite Colorado. Well, as contrite as a smirking Colorado could get.

"There will be no talking about emus on this flight," Vlad ordered.

We all nodded, and behind his back, Colorado was

biting his lip. He wasn't taking the not-to-be-spoken-about-incident seriously, but I doubt there was anything that would make him take things seriously in any kind of genuine way. Music, sex, and hockey, that was his life, and I didn't know how he was even still alive. I did know his drug tests always came back clean and he was sober, but if all you have to live for were hockey, music and sex, then what kind of future did you have?

Vlad glanced around the cabin and our gazes locked for a millisecond, nowhere near long enough for me to send him a reassuring smile, or to do anything to make him feel better.

"Sit!" he ordered Colorado, and pointed at the seat next to him.

"Iceman, hell no, I need to be in my lucky seat."

Vlad reared up over him, and then shoved him none too gently into the seat before taking the one next to him. "You don't need luck if you're not playing," he snapped. I'm not sure he meant for the entire plane to hear him, but we did.

Were we really going to face Calgary with Andre in goal, who was barely out of diapers in a hockey-goalie sense, when we could have had Colorado and maybe pulled a win out of our asses?

"We're fucked," Andre groaned under his breath, but Ryker elbowed him in the side.

"Dude, we got this," he reassured him.

WE SO HADN'T GOT THIS.

Four goals against and we'd fought back, but their

goalie was better than ours and that was just in the first period. When the horn sounded after that first twenty minutes I'd never been so relieved. The JAR line had tried, my line had tried, our third and fourth lines had pushed hard, but we couldn't get anything by the big Czech in the Calgary net, and Vlad's defense pair were on the ice so much he was exhausted. Getting back into the locker room, we wore a defeated air, going through the motions and living up to our label of worst team in the whole freaking league.

Colorado was suited up, our backup, benched, and I genuinely thought that even with the whole emu incident that he would be put in goal. I think he'd expected it too.

Coach Carmichael paced around the logo in the center of the locker room, thin-lipped and tight with tension.

"Okay," he began, and exchanged glances with Assistant Coach Anderson, who leaned back against the wall and nodded before he continued. "I actually saw some good work out there."

I could feel the surprise in the room. Next to me Alex huffed.

"Four goals Andre let in," he continued, and I felt so damn sorry for the kid who looked wiped out. "The first one, yeah, that was on him, he was too far out of his crease, and he knows it." He glanced at Andre.

"Yes, Coach." Andre sounded broken, as if it was all too much for him.

"Goal two, what the hell were you even doing that far back Alex?"

Alex blinked up at Coach, "I was—"

"Goal three, Vlad, Eli, you were screening so badly that Andre couldn't get line of sight. Why was that?"

Vlad stiffened. "With respect—"

"And four, well, our penalty kill team, I mean, what the fuck, Ryker? Eli? Tate? Do we not run enough drills?"

By now we'd all come to realize he wasn't *actually* looking for answers at all.

"Let Andre do his job," He held up a board, a complicated mess of Os and Xs that made sense to all of us. "Vlad, the D, I want you away from him, stop blocking him, he doesn't need your help with that, I want you chasing down their forwards, got it?"

"Coach," All of the D-men replied as one. Captain or not, if Vlad had fucked up then he was happy to be told.

"JAR line, Tate, your line, they have a solid defense blocking your way, I'm switching you up, confusing the shit out of them, I'm putting Tate, Alex and Ryker out first, with the remaining fifty-two seconds of this penalty kill. I want to see speed, accuracy, and I want any penalty they might get, made deader than an emu."

"I think you meant dodo," Colorado piped up and deflated when Coach glared at him.

"Vlad?" he prompted.

Then it was Vlad's turn to talk. I was sure he'd say something inspiring in as few words as he could. That was his way; he knew what to say and when to say it, that was why he was the captain and that was why we all listened to him. My eyes slipped south to the floor and back up again as I recalled the way he'd held me against the refrigerator, and I was instantly getting hard, which in a cup was damn uncomfortable.

"Do we want to finish at the bottom of the league this year?"

Silence, and then a soft chorus of noes, including me.

"Do we want to make it to the Stanley Cup Finals?"

This time the confirmations came faster, but I sensed doubt in the tone, and Coach frowned at Vlad. The Raptors making it halfway up the table would be something to aim for. I was good, Ryker was good, Alex, Sebastian, Colorado when he wasn't being a complete asshole, we could get up there, we just needed faith.

"Do you want to beat this team?"

"Hell, yes," Ryker snapped next to me, a little louder than everyone else.

Vlad nodded at him. "Clean. Play the game. Keep your eyes open. Do not crowd Andre. And most of all, get some shots on goal. Got me?"

The reply was a chorus of "Yes Captain!" and it was loud and purposeful. We knew what we were doing wrong, and it was time to go out and beat Calgary.

Of course, we didn't make it easy on ourselves. We managed to cut their four-goal lead, two from me, two from Ryker, and a beautiful slapshot from Eli. We tied at five each, took it to overtime, but we all knew that Andre would be out of his element in goal. He tried so damn hard, but Calgary got that decisive goal and won the two points. Still, we left with a point for tying the game, and you bet it was the best feeling in the entire damn world. With all the high-fiving going on I thought I'd be able to do the same to Vlad, but he'd given a speech telling us we rocked, before making his excuses and tugging Colorado out of the locker room.

We were staying at the Regency, a twenty-minute coach ride to the arena, and by the time we reached our rooms we'd dissected every penalty, every goal, each tiny play, and even Vlad had joined us, although he never once looked at me or talked to me directly.

I was exhausted, elated, concerned that Vlad and I had been nothing but a one-night stand, and now I was in my tiny hotel room, and thank God the whole sharing-rooms thing from my college days had been and gone. I showered, paced, checked for any news on emus, watched the replays of the game that were beginning to show up, checked the Tate Collins hashtag for any more Lacey news, and that was it.

There was nothing for it, but to go to bed, and think about how maybe, *just maybe,* messing around with Vlad in his kitchen had been a very bad thing.

Chapter Eight

Vlad

SENSIBLE: A COURSE OF ACTION CHOSEN WITH PRUDENCE.

That was how the dictionary explained the one word that I'd always tried to base my actions on. I was not one to be rash or rush into things. That was more my brother Dimi. I was the cool one, the levelheaded twin, the man who approached a problem systematically and with control. If you lost restraint you did foolish things. Things that could harm you in ways you never imagined when you were being a moron. My brother Dimi and the farm pond incident when we were twelve sprang to mind.

He had insisted that the ice on the small farm pond we played pick-up games on was thick enough after one or two cold nights. Papa had warned us off the pond just the day before. So, being bullheaded, Dimi skated out, turned to look at me and gave me the shish, an old Russian hand gesture with the thumb between the middle and index finger. It was a childish gesture that we always used when we were arguing. No sooner had he finished lifting his hand had the ice broken under him. He'd lost his new skates and had to slop home soaking wet with chattering teeth and explain to Papa where his skates were. Not a sensible lad my brother.

Now, it seemed, I was beginning to act like my reckless twin. Even as I made the call I knew I was being careless, but the drive to see him was too strong to be ignored.

Tate picked up on the fifth ring as I placed a dress shoe between the door and the frame to keep it from closing and locking immediately.

"Hey there," he said, my ear instantly pleased with the sound of Texas caressing it.

"Hello. Come to my room. Bring your digital playbook."

"I…uhm…what?"

"Come to my room. Bring a digital playbook. Be here within ten minutes. The door is propped open. Bring the shoe inside with you."

I ended the call, leaned back in the short-backed gray chair by the standard hotel room desk, and picked up my drink. Three fingers of Stoli with a twist of orange over two cubes. Hotel mini bars were a marvel. The heater clicked on, stirring up the dry air. I sipped my vodka. Would he come? Would he not? I hoped so. The past two days babysitting an out-of-control rock star/goalie had worn on my jagged nerves. I wanted to spend time with Tate. See where he was mentally, feel out how far he was willing to go in this slow dance of dominance and submission. He would have to bend to my wishes if he wanted in my bed. God knows I desired him as my lover, as stupid as that was. A sharp rap on the door made me smile. I glanced at the silver Rolex on my wrist. Seven minutes. Impressive. I called for him to enter.

My pulse kicked up. There was a short hallway he had to come down, passing the bathroom to gain access to the room and bed. When he cleared the corner, I smiled at him over my drink. He was in lounge pants and a tank top with a clam on the front, his feet in sneakers. In his hands was an iPad and my black dress shoe. He gave the room a once over, found me in the corner by the drawn draperies, and flashed that sweet-as-apple-pie smile. It made my already hard cock ache.

"So I brought the tablet, but don't you have one of your own?" He took a few steps closer. I held up my left hand to stop him.

"Take off your clothes," I said, surprised at the timbre of my voice. His brown eyes flared. "Take off your clothes." He looked around as if expecting Colorado or Ryker to jump out and yell "Gotcha!" but no one was here but us. "Take. Off. Your. Clothes."

I saw the giddy nervousness creep into his gaze. "You're serious?"

"I am always serious. I do not want to ask again. Take off your clothes. Slowly," I added when he tossed the tablet and shoe to the bedside table and yanked at his tank top. "Slowly. Strip for me. Make me want you."

"What are we doing, an LGBT remake of *True Lies* or what?" He joked nervously.

"I don't know what you're talking about."

He rolled his eyes. "Watch a movie sometime. *True Lies*? Arnold and Jamie Lee? She does that sexy strip tease for Arnold who's sitting in a chair and—never mind. I don't know…you want me to like shake my ass or just get naked?"

"Take off your clothes slowly then come to me on your hands and knees."

His eyes went wider, but he liked what I was suggesting. I could see it in the way he wet his lips and began moving, lifting his shirt up inch by inch, baring his abs then his chest. His tiny nipples were hard. My tongue ached to flick them. I took another sip of vodka and watched the show. He wasn't going to win any awards for sensual movements, but then again he was a big, muscular hockey player, not a lithe dancer.

When he stood there nude, I ran my gaze over him, lingering on his thighs and hard cock then moving up over his stomach to his face. His pupils were blown already. Oh yes, he liked this sort of dynamic.

"Come to me. Crawl over. Put your cheek on my groin, resting your nose against my dick." I was surprised at how smooth my voice sounded. My heart was thumping. Tate went down with more grace than he'd shown during his impromptu striptease. Eyes locked on me, Tate made his way to me on his hands and knees. I spread my legs for him when he drew close. He never hesitated as he wiggled between my thighs and put his cheek on my erection. I placed my left hand to his head, pushed gently, and rubbed my cock against his nose and lips. He gasped, turning his head just so to nibble at my length. I rocked up more, pushing against his lips. His tongue darted out and I came close to dropping my drink. "Enough. Pick up your head."

He did. I slid my free hand around the back of his neck and lifted him upward, pulling him over me, his bare chest lying against my clothed one. He opened for me the moment my lips touched his. God above, he was made for me. His mouth tasted sweet, like soda pop. I swept in deep. He met me stroke for stroke, soft little moans of pleasure sneaking out of his mouth when I'd tip his head this way or that.

"Vlad," he gasped, the sound of my name on that hot exhalation nearly had me coming in my pants. That was not happening. Tonight, I was coming inside him.

"Mm, such a beautiful man you are," I purred, nipping down his jaw to his neck where I sucked and bit until he was whimpering. "Get on the bed."

I released him, hoping to gain a little lost control when he left me. That never happened. Seeing Tate spreading himself across the massive king-sized bed, ass in the air, was more than I could take. I tossed back my vodka, reached for my small toiletry bag that held shaving supplies, my toothbrush, and comb, as well as condoms and lube, and was resting by my chair, and got to my feet.

His ragged breaths filled the room. I reached out with a finger, trailing it down the crack of his ass. He jerked and whined, muttering something about losing his mind.

"Do you want me to take you like this, from behind?" I cupped his balls. He pulled in a long breath between his teeth. "Is it what you want?"

"I…yeah… maybe. It's on the gay porn that I've seen."

Smiling, I rolled his heavy sac. "Did you always watch gay porn?"

"Maybe."

That confession made me smile even wider. Of course he did. "I do too when I feel the itch. Do you jerk off to it?"

"Sometimes." He moved his hips side to side. I patted a cheek, kneaded the bubble butt that was so like mine and every other hockey player I knew. "God, can we...do something?"

"We are. You're telling me things that are pleasing me and I'm pleasing you. So, are you sure you want your first time from behind?" His tiny little hole was tempting me, so I ran a finger around the edges. He gasped and jerked. "If I take you this way it will feel deeper."

"Okay deep, yeah, deep is good. Yeah? Or no, I...fuck I don't know." He pushed back against my finger, eager, or so he thought. "I want you in me."

A shudder of want raced down my spine. I flicked open the lube and coated his ass crack, working the slick down over his entrance, over his balls, and slathering his leaky cock. He groaned long and low when I worked the lube over his prick. As I stroked with my left hand I began working a finger into him. His moans were like hymns, sweet and heavenly. He never once pulled away; if anything he was *too* greedy for the penetration.

"More," he huffed after I had my middle finger all the way in. I bent down to nip at his ass cheek, then worked another finger in, all the while tugging on his prick. Precum ran out of him, adding to the slip and slide. "More, fuck. Oh, shit...I...shit!"

I chuckled and tapped his prostate again. "Did none of your women ever do this for you?"

"No. I…fuck! Stop, stop…it's too close."

I pulled my fingers out and began taking off my clothes, item by item, tossing them on the bed beside him. He watched as my jeans, underwear, socks, and T-shirt landed right beside him.

"You're going to love this after you adjust," I whispered as I tore open a foil packet and rolled the condom down over me. "It will make you sore though, I cannot stop that but I do have something for your ass when I'm done with it. I'll take care of you, *zvedva moya.*"

My star. That was what I'd called him and that was what he was. A brilliant body… a blessing from a goddess. And he was mine. All six-foot-plus of him. He knew it and I did as well. I eased a knee up onto the bed, then another, and used them to spread him wider. His fingernails raked over the wooden headboard.

"You'll want to breathe," I whispered as I pressed my cockhead against his ass. He eased back as I pushed. My head was buried in him. He tensed, his hands finding purchase on the edge of the headboard. "Breathe, good, good, yes, pretty man. So pretty. So bright. *Zvedva moya,* my star. Breathe, yes…yes…yes."

The tension lessened. I pushed in deeper and deeper, inch by inch, until he had all of me inside him, just as he'd begged for.

"Oh fuck, fuck…I… don't move, I just…fuck," he huffed.

I pulled out just a bit then slid back in. He grunted. I did it again, and again, and again, until he was arching his spine to take more. Only then did I release his hips and slap my hands to his chest, jerking him back to me, his back to my chest. He cried out. I took his cock in hand as I pumped. His head fell to the side, baring his throat. I fell on his neck like a vampire just freed from its crypt. Biting and sucking, I feasted on him as we fucked.

"Give me...your mouth," I growled. He turned his head and I saw his face. Flushed and sweaty, eyes nothing but black, mouth parted. Such a beautiful face. I licked into his open mouth, the kiss sloppy and wet, my hips moving faster and faster. "Come for me now. Let go. Come for me, my sweet star."

He blew apart at my command. Hot jets of cum coating my hand and the bedding. I worked him, milking him dry, and then rocked up to bury myself as deep as I could. Sparks raced up my spine as my orgasm hit. He reached back with both hands to grab at my hips and ass to keep me where I was. Cock kicking, I lurched and groaned, kissing him with passion. He met each hungry swipe of my tongue with his own.

We tasted each other forever, the kisses softening. Just like my cock. I eased out of his body, my arms still around him, and we both fell face first into the bed.

"Holy shit," he murmured, his face buried in a thick pillow. I rolled off the bed after giving his ass a pat. "You're a fucking beast."

That made me chuckle as I tied off the condom and dropped it into the trash can by the desk. Turning, I took a moment to enjoy the sight of a well-fucked Tate Collins in my bed, belly down, legs splayed, his gorgeous ass bearing a love bite. I wanted to cover him with marks. Let the world and all the other horny bastards and bitches know that he belonged to someone. And that someone was not one who shared well. Or at all.

He rolled to his back when I climbed into the bed, his eyes glowing. I stole a kiss, then gathered him into my arms, flopping backward, taking him with me. He lay on top of me now, his prick still leaking, his body pink and damp.

"This is something either very bad or very good," I said, staring into his eyes. His brows tangled. "I hope it will be good but there are so many things that may make it bad."

"Yeah, I know." He pushed up to sit on my thighs and winced. "Ouch, okay, fuck, my ass aches."

"We will tend to that momentarily."

A flimsy smile pulled at his mouth. "Novocain for my ass?"

"No, asshole cream for an asshole."

"Will you use your dick to work it up inside me?"

He looked nothing like the All-American boy the league touted him as. He was rumpled, marked, covered with semen and sweat, and asking for another ass fucking by his male captain. If the Raptors PR people could've seen Mr. Sweet as Apple Pie now they'd have been flabbergasted.

"No, not again tonight. A few fingers though…" That brought out his dazzling smile. "Tate, this relationship that we're having. You must know that I am not an easy man to be with. We must not allow our love affair to become public. My family is vulnerable back in Russia. I know

Americans are all for being out and proud, and I wish I could be, perhaps later but right now I—"

He bent down to put his lips to mine. A soft, silencing kiss. "It's fine. We'll keep us to us. Maybe just some friends." My eyes flared. "The team already knows or suspects. Strongly. Colorado sees the way I look at you, or you at me, or maybe he just has some sort of sixth sense about people having the hots for other people."

"Do not speak of Colorado to me tonight while we are being close. It sours my mood," I grumbled. He spread himself over me like a big, heavy man blanket. "He is the biggest hemorrhoid in the National Hockey League."

"Yeah, he's got some fire in him," Tate sighed, his cheek on my pectoral. "He's a free spirit and you're Mr. Control so you two are bound to rub each other wrong."

"Hmm," I replied, my fingers moving up and down his spine as our skin began to dry and cool. "Well, I am not a funny man."

"I think you're hilarious."

"Your thoughts will change in a short time. I'm strict and controlling, in bed and out."

"Yeah, I noticed. I kind of dig you telling me to take off my clothes and all that shit."

I smiled despite myself. "That's good. I dislike men in my bed who are pushy and toppy. That is my role." He hummed like a contented cat. "I am troublesome though. I must have order. Neatness, control, and many men find that irritating."

"We'll work on loosening you up a bit, Iceberg."

"Pfft."

"First thing we're going to do is order us up some junk food, shower, find that ass cream of yours, and watch us some superhero movies." He kissed my nipple, then wiggled free, his feet hitting the floor at the same time he grimaced. "Jesus, you damn Russian plow horse." He tenderly reached around to touch his ass. I had a small moment of pride as most men would, being likened to a horse. "Maybe ass cream first, *then* food, followed by Marvel movies."

"Superhero films are silly. Who wears capes and spandex?" I inquired as I rolled out of bed and gathered him to me. "Why do we not watch something with some substance that will make our brains work?"

"Oh my God, don't tell me you're an arthouse fan?"

"Perhaps. Sue me for seeking out intelligent entertainment."

He took my face in his hands. "We're going to have to work on getting you looser."

"I plan to do that to you," I whispered then captured his mouth. He sighed into the kiss and somehow we ended up back in bed, minus any food or movies until well after two in the morning. I did tend to his sore bottom with ample cream. Then came mutual hand jobs, a long shared shower, and a last minute call to room service for chicken tenders, curly French fries, and root beer. Which I placed as the taste on his mouth when he'd first arrived. Root beer.

He was lying beside me, feeding a long spiral fry into my mouth as *Guardians of the Galaxy* was playing on his phone, which was propped up on a pillow resting on my stomach.

"I like this Drax," I said after we'd clocked an hour of movie time. Perhaps not *all* superhero films were bad.

"That's because you and he are the same person," he said around his mouthful of curly fry.

He fell asleep with his head on my chest. I ran my fingers over his cheekbones, wishing I could close my eyes and drift off to a talking raccoon shooting a huge gun. But that was not to be.

"Tate, you cannot be here in the morning," I said, giving him a shake after the movie ended. He sat up, looked around groggily, and then nodded. "I'm sorry. It is not as I would wish it."

"Nah, it's cool. We both have far too much bullshit to deal with in our lives right now. We don't need the media nightmare that Tennant Rowe suffered through." He slid from the bed, taking his phone with him, and pulled on his clothes. I'd been the one to answer the door when room service came and had left my jeans on after the food had arrived.

"Do you want the leftover food?" I held up the plate that held only two out of thirty tenders. He shook his head then tugged his tank top on. "I do wish you could stay. Waking up with you would be nice."

"Yeah, it would. Maybe when we're back home without nosy coaches and teammates right across the hall?"

"That would be fine, most fine." He gave me a soft, fleeting kiss. I handed him his iPad, walked him to the door, peeked out to see if the coast were clear, and then let him step out into the hall. "See you at breakfast."

"Yeah, cool. Thanks for…well, thanks." He moved as

if he sought another kiss and I almost capitulated. It was the *ping* of the elevator down the hall that kept me from pressing him to the wall for another kiss or, worse yet, leading him back to my bed.

"Good night," I said, smiled feebly, and closed the door on him. I'd had many lovers, all on the sly, but saying goodbye to Tate was by far the hardest farewell I'd ever experienced. I yearned for him already.

Obviously, caution had flown the proverbial coop.

Chapter Nine

Tate

OUR GAME AGAINST VANCOUVER WAS A SHIT SHOW. IT was chaotic, nasty, pushing, shoving, hell, and when we finally left the ice with a five-two loss, it was a relief more than a shock. Vancouver were hot this season, winning all of their games so far, and jeez, did Canada love that one. The signs in the arena were deadly accurate, including the first appearance of the SHT line poster with the little 'I' in the middle.

"I think the Zamboni got me," Andre dragged himself from the shower, and I couldn't see bruises yet, but some of the one hundred mile an hour pucks had hit him hard, and twice he'd been steamrolled by the D, plus a whole heap of his own team who were losing their shit and trying to keep the puck out of our net. In Andre's defense, he'd put up a good fight, and I didn't think Colorado could have done any better.

"That last save, dude, that was insane," I high-fived

him as he passed, and at least he smiled, before he winced again. How he'd seen that puck and gotten across the crease as fast as he did, I don't know, but it had been awesome to see, a glimpse of a wonderful future.

Alex had dropped gloves with one of the Vancouver D, but the fight hadn't lasted long and it was Alex on the ice with the D sitting on him. After that incident, penalties served, the JAR line had never found its footing, and my line deserved the moniker of SHiT.

Andre didn't bother dressing, the team doctor taking him off. A couple of the guys headed for post-game cool down on bikes, and Alex was definitely limping.

What the fuck? We weren't even at Christmas, and we'd lost all sense of who we were out there on the ice.

Vlad was quiet in his cubicle, his blond head dipped, still in his skates and rhythmically tapping a finger on his knee. I had this insane urge to go over and ask him if he was okay, but then they called for interviews, and it was him, me, and Alex who were called in.

I couldn't hear what they were asking Vlad, but I could hear his answers, which were standard replies about not playing the Raptors game, and how lessons would be learned, and congratulating Vancouver on a decisive win.

Alex was way over the other side of the room, attempting to front the fact he'd lost a fight with a D-Man almost twice his size.

And me? I was getting asked a whole ton of shit. After seven years I was used to this, some interviewers asked searching questions that called on the skater to think hard, but tonight this had had the smell of failure.

"Did you mean to turn over the puck at the end of the second?"

"Does anyone mean to do that?" I tried for funny, and then read the crowd. "We all make mistakes, but we learn from them. That was entirely on me."

"Do you think the investment in you is a good move for the Raptors?"

Shit. The money question, like are you actually worth 23.1 million? "Our team is working well. Learning to adapt." Take that for avoidance.

"Did you expect to come in and make a distinctive change in the team?"

"The team is strong; you haven't see us at our best yet."

"Why haven't you made a difference?"

Christ, this was back to the headlines when apparently I was coming to the Raptors to save the team. They didn't need saving, and I hated the assumption that me landing in Arizona would be some kind of freaking salvation. I was good, but the whole team had to be good. And tonight, I'd played like shit.

"We're working hard," was all I said.

"Are the troubles you had in Dallas following you here?" One wily reporter thrust the microphone at my face, with a gleam in their eye, and I was this close to expecting a question about Tennant Rowe.

"No."

I sent a quick glance toward our media rep after I'd managed to answer everything that I was prepared to, and she moved between me and them, and used all manner of persuasion to push them back.

"Tate! Are you aware that your fiancée is—?"

I turned and walked away. *Former* fiancée, and I was done with tonight.

I didn't go to Vlad's room, he didn't ask me to, but then he'd locked himself away with Coach Carmichael and Colorado, and no doubt shit was going to hit the fan soon anyway. The game tonight, Colorado and his freaking emu and fuck knows what else, and Alex's limp diagnosed as a pulled muscle, which might pull him out of the final Canada game in Toronto.

Could things get any worse?

The flight from Calgary to Toronto was long and tedious and so very quiet. Not a lot of card-playing, or guys with their hand-held game machines trying to kill each other, just the infrequent buzz of chatter. Alex was slumped in his seat, earbuds in, eyes shut. Colorado was hemmed in by Vlad who was looking ahead with his icy, stony expression, Ryker and Eli had iPads out, Ryker probably contacting Jacob, and I knew Eli was studying for a degree and only had a few credits left he needed to attain. I'd heard from Henry, who had it from Ryker, who'd been told by Sam, that Kricker the emu was now in a better place—a wildlife sanctuary on the outskirts of Tucson, and there was the very real possibility that Colorado was getting a fine for owning an emu which was on the Arizona no-go list.

Trying not to focus on that, or the lack of sexy Russian in any bed anywhere, I put headphones on and selected a random playlist, Muse merging with Kings of Leon, and then changing to Queen and Pink Floyd. I liked the prog rock bands, with soaring lyrics, and an edge to the music, and even though I wasn't fully into the kind of music that Colorado made, he had a touch of clever words and heavy beats, close enough to some of my favorites that I would've loved to see his band play one day.

Of course, that was if he wasn't in prison for owning an illegal pet in the state of Arizona.

It was late when we landed, and still no call from Vlad to go to his room. After jerking off in the shower, and then jerking off a couple of hours after to the memories of what we'd done, I pulled together the courage to text him, a simple, *wanna talk about the game?* No one could think that was anything other than one teammate reaching out to another, but he replied thirty-two minutes later with a simple *not tonight.*

Fuck knows what that was about.

Our free day in Toronto was all about the CN Tower, dinner, six of us attempting to not look like hockey players all standing on the glass walkway of the tower and staring down at the large whale painted on the roof of the Aquarium. The yellow sign said the glass would take the weight of three-point-five Orcas, which of course led to teasing about weight, particularly when it came to the part about the glass holding the weight of one thousand and ninety-one beavers, which we all found hilarious. This wasn't my first time up the tower, and I was confident to stand in the middle and watch through the clouds as they cleared and passed by to reveal the tiny ant-like people below, but it was my first time with new friends, and I loved it.

Of course we got recognized, took selfies with fans, signed some autographs, and received some gentle teasing about being Raptors. But I had the one that would go down in history as the worst place to be recognized—in the bathroom, for God's sake. Given I was holding my dick and taking a piss when the guy said hi, it was kind of unfortunate, but at least he and I laughed over not having a pen available. One pair of washed hands later, I found out that he was a Calgary fan, and my stomach fell. We exchanged notes on the Calgary game and I stayed ever so polite and I didn't once call him an opinionated asshole when he called my line the SHiT line.

I even shook his hand, and when I joined the guys who were waiting in the gift shop trying on hats, they took one look at me and they must have known.

"You were ages," Ryker commented, yanking at the cap which couldn't quite contain his soft fluffy bangs unless he pushed them up and under.

"Calgary fan," was all I said.

They nodded in silent understanding, then changed the subject. It was how we dealt.

At least Vlad came to dinner with us in the evening, but he wouldn't glance my way or indeed anyone, and he had this grumpy Russian thing going on. Colorado was subdued, and Coach Carmichael was trying his best to get the group into a happy space.

Tomorrow was an afternoon game with Toronto. On a Saturday. Kids, lots of kids, family, and you could bet the arena would be heaving. This, after all, was the home to the Hall of Fame, and the fans were dedicated.

I just wished that Vlad would… what? Come to my room, text me to go to his to talk strategy, at least give me the benefit of at least acknowledging me. Because if he didn't, then did that mean it had been a one-night thing? Were we done at one fuck and a blowjob, and other interesting things?

We were good against Toronto, in fact better than good. The SHT line wasn't quite as shit as the Toronto fans had hoped. With Alex out with his lower body injury, Sam moved up to the JAR line, and somehow they clicked, and we had Lewis, one of our third line and we clicked as well. It was poetry, and we drew level at two goals each with only three minutes left in the game. Vlad was an animal, he was everywhere, he was large and intimidating, Andre was laser focused, Ryker was a freaking genius and got our first goal, our penalty kill rocked, and I scored the second goal.

Take that, interviewers who think I'm shit and not worth being a Raptor.

The clock ticked down. We wanted the full two points. All we needed to do was get one more goal, just one, and we'd have a clear win. In Toronto. Everything was amped up to the max, and weirdly slowed down all at the same time. I got the tap to take my line over and we hit the ice just as Toronto lost control of the puck, a turnover from an exhausted forward, and Vlad had it for a second, hitting it hard to the boards so it flew around the net, straight to my stick. It didn't stay there for long, a no-look pass to Henry because I knew he'd be there, Lewis was close to the net, waiting for Henry to shuttle the puck to him. The Toronto goalie had his eyes on Lewis, a scrappy front of net fighter, and he'd made a rookie mistake, taking his eyes off me.

Henry feinted a pass to Lewis, sent it careening to me instead, and with the goalie out of position I slammed that puck so hard it sent the goalie's water bottle flying. The lamp lit and there was no call against the goal. We were three-two up, and there were twenty-seven seconds on the clock.

Toronto pulled their goalie for the next face-off, left their net exposed and replaced the goalie with another forward, but it wasn't enough. We didn't get an empty net goal, but we sure as hell got a win.

And it was the best freaking thing in the entire damn world.

Dinner was at this pizzeria that Alex knew, and he was there waiting for us, congratulating us on the win, pissed he couldn't have been part of it, but so happy for us all. We were on a high, and everything was lit up in my head. I even got a smile from Vlad and a fist bump with an added nod of encouragement. I wonder if maybe tonight I would get a call? Just at the thought of it I was half hard, and he knew.

The food was great, the conversation great, everything was *great.*

Only, halfway through dinner, Ryker's phone lit up, and he looked at the messages and then up at me. Then Sam's phone lit up, then Henry's. We were all connected in a group chat, but my phone hadn't vibrated in my pocket, so this wasn't a group chat post, or a joke, or some stupid Tik-Tok video guaranteed to have me snorting with laughter.

"Tate," Ryker caught my gaze and held it, and my chest tightened. Was this some Tennant Rowe shit blowing up in my face? Hell, was it Ten himself messaging his stepson? I understood the silent message that I should check my phone and had to wriggle against Eli who grumbled and teased and made some comment about me touching his thigh.

"In your dreams," I muttered, and he elbowed me in the side.

I wasn't sure what I was looking for, but I didn't have to go far. I had a long list of messages on Instagram and over three hundred twitter notifications commenting on a link. When I clicked the twitter link it was direct to a heartfelt essay on Lacey's hockey-girlfriend's blog, the one she'd dedicated all her time to when I was back down south and she was still my fiancée in that damn live show. The headline was enough to have me scrambling to stand in horror, in shock, in a new kind of hell.

Sometimes you don't even know the abuse is happening.

Chapter Ten

Vlad

THE FLIGHT BACK TO ARIZONA WAS RIFE WITH TENSION. As soon as we'd piled onto the charter jet the anxiety among the players was obvious. Tate sat by himself in the back, burrowed into his own private hell. I longed to leave my seat across from Colorado and go to him, take him in my arms, settle him protectively on my lap, and reassure him that all would be well. I could not do that though. For several reasons. One being that I had promised Coach I'd keep a short leash on Penn, who was fidgety already. Lack of groupies, or so I imagined. The second reason was the most obvious one.

Pulling my sexy teammate into my lap in public just might be considered a declaration of my gay status, something that was not on my To-Do list. And thirdly, I remained in my seat because I wasn't sure if the accusation Tate's ex-fiancée had made against him had any merit. Yes, I knew Tate Collins biblically, but I didn't know the man well at all. And what did that say about me? My mother would be shamed. Papa, I think, would understand, as he had had sown many wild oats before settling down with Mama.

"Dude, please, you are taxing my creative vibe with your negative energy output," Colorado grumbled, looking up from the acoustic guitar he'd been plucking. "Just go talk to him."

"I have no idea—"

"Oh, yeah, right, we're repressing our inner queer. Whatever." He waved a hand, the gaudy thumb ring catching the sun's reflection. "Just take all your broody, angst-filled, Final Fantasy junk to some other seat. I'm a grown man, I don't need a babysitter."

"Management disagrees."

That made him chuckle. "Yeah, well, you can't have management without man."

I stared at him across the card table. "Obviously."

"No, Iceman, man as in '*The Man*', you know?" When I said nothing he tossed his shaggy hair from his face, his attention leaving me to focus solely on the guitar.

The song was a slow one, his voice craggy and smoky, working with the lyrics perfectly. The chatter on the plane fell off as the men all sat back to enjoy Penn's newest song. He sang of braying dogs, winter moons, and the pines that scraped the window as he held his man close. What would it be like to be so open about one's sexuality? I so envied Colorado that. The man was blatant in his admiration of both sexes, happy to tell whoever would listen that he was not one to be jammed into boxes, proudly wearing the pansexual colors whenever possible. I threw a glance to the back, attention skimming over Ryker and Alex, then touching on Henry. All three men were involved with other men, Ryker planning to wed his man soon.

My gaze landed on Tate, who had lifted his sad eyes from his phone to watch Colorado play his power ballad. Our eyes met and held. Did I dare go to him? What would people think? Would Coach berate me for abandoning my duties to console my…teammate/lover/possibly more.

"Dude, just go to him," Colorado whispered during a break in the lyrics. I blinked. He gave his head a small jerk in Tate's direction.

I rose almost as if I had no control over my legs. Like a puppet I stood and walked stiff-legged down the aisle, not looking left or right until I got to the back row. Tate's gaze had never left mine as I'd closed the distance.

"May I sit?" I asked cautiously. It felt quite similar. I could feel the men on the plane watching me. The weight of their curiosity sat on my shoulders like cement blocks. My stomach flipped, my palms damp.

"Sure," Tate replied in a soft, surprised manner. I dropped beside him, not across from him as a friend would. Or would a friend sit beside him? Was I being too gay? "You look like I feel."

My gaze flew from the card table to Tate. "I feel as if you should not ride home alone."

"I didn't do it. What she said…I would never hurt anyone. Ever. She's upset and she has every right to be. I just… I want you to know that. The guys are all funny now, like they want to believe me but they have doubts. I can't… " He tore his sight from mine to stare at the clouds below us. "I can't have *you* thinking I'm that kind of man."

Damn this world and the ones who used others for their own game. If we'd been home I could've reached out and touched him, held him in my arms, eased the pain that poured off him. I peered up the aisle, searching for what I should say or do next, and met the languid gaze of Colorado Penn. He gave me a peace sign, laughed at the song request that Ryker had called out, and then began playing 'Jet Airliner' by Steve Miller. It was one of the songs that was always requested during a flight, closely followed by Coach asking for anything by the Eagles. As the men sang about hearts called backwards I placed my hand atop Tate's as it rested on his knee. His eyes flew from the clouds to my face, seeking something. I squeezed his fingers, just once, and lightly, but left my hand there.

"Thanks," he whispered, the lines around his mouth lessening a little. That was how we made the rest of the flight, my hand on his. Most of the men couldn't see it, no one even knew, but if felt monumental to me. Tate relayed horror story after horror story to me about his time with Lacey as we winged across the states. By the time we landed at TIA any doubts I may have had about him had been wiped away. I felt bad for ever doubting the man, as his grief was palpable.

We'd only just landed when two men in cheap suits appeared from the terminal, badges flashing. Tate stiffened at my side.

"Mr. Collins, Detectives Polkowski and Harrison, Tucson Police Department. We'd like to ask you a few questions about assertions that have been made against you by a Ms. Lacey Mason. Regarding an incident of alleged aggravated assault that took place two months ago."

Tate began to stammer. I edged around him as the team began to gather in a circle around us to listen.

"Are you arresting him?" The two police officers gave me that look. It said I should shut up and get out of their faces. "If you are not arresting him he does not have to go with you."

"Are you his lawyer?" The tall cop, Harrison, asked me as his partner, the shorter, heavier one, was talking at Tate. Coach had waded through the crowd of players, and was now jawing at the pale cop.

"No, I am his team captain and his friend."

"Ah well then, you need to step back and let us talk with Mr. Collins."

"I will do no such thing," I replied, squaring my shoulders.

"Vlad, no, it's cool. I'll go with them. I have nothing to hide," Tate stated with confidence.

I threw a glance at Coach.

"We'll have someone from legal meet you. Don't say anything until you have counsel, Tate," Coach Carmichael said as the cops were already steering Tate toward a gold sedan.

I followed the unmarked car all the way to the downtown police station. The tan brick building was large and a bit confusing. I ended up sitting on a hard wooden bench next to a water cooler for two hours. In that time I grew more than agitated, I grew pissed off as the Americans liked to say. No one in this massive place would answer any of my questions about Tate. I had no idea where he was, if a lawyer had arrived, if they were arresting him, or if they'd already thrown him in a cell where he would rot and none of us would ever see him again. I had to remind myself that America did not do such things. I paced, I cursed, I railed at whoever would listen, and then I was finally asked to wait outside or I was going to be spending some time in a cell to cool off. Four hours passed in total before Tate emerged from the police station with a short, fat man in a blue suit. Both appeared exhausted.

How I didn't race up to him and hug him I would never know. I met him at the curb. He gave me a weary smile. His attorney was talking a mile a minute, his high brow breaking out in a damp sweat.

"Go home and don't speak to anyone from the press. Ms. Mason is already suggesting her assertions we taken out of context, the police know that, and given your agreeable nature and willingness to talk with them I think this could be done and dusted by tomorrow. Meanwhile, the media is gorging on her vague social media posts and it's a feeding frenzy. Keep your head down, don't engage in any kind of outlandish behavior, no social media, and we'll get this fixed."

"Thank you, Mr. Morton." Tate and his lawyer shook hands, I nodded at the man as he passed. I'd seen him around the arena, mostly in his dealing with Penn. I didn't envy our legal department or the owners anything. This team was a handful that even I had trouble keeping in line.

"My car is here." I led Tate to my blue Audi. "We will go back to the airport to get your car."

"I took an Uber," he replied wearily falling into the

passenger seat as soon as I unlocked the doors with my fob. "Why did you drive to the airport and then pay to park?"

"I don't like others driving," I replied as I slid behind the wheel after tossing his bag into the trunk.

"Control freak," he muttered, then scrubbed at his face. "Just when I think my life is getting back in shape, more shit hits the fan."

I nodded. What else could I say? He was right. Life was nothing but shit splattering through fans.

"The lawyer sounds optimistic," I said as I backed out of my parking slot and eased into late afternoon traffic.

"I didn't do it. I wasn't even around on the dates she said it happened. I just... I cannot *believe* she made an official complaint! Like, what the fuck!"

He railed and shouted and punched his thighs the whole way home. He was still steaming mad when we stopped at my neighbors' to pick up Frank. Tom and his wife had an African Gray called Molly, and so were well acquainted with parrot care. Frank and Molly were friends, and enjoyed each other's company, so Tom and Mona were my parrot sitters when I traveled.

Frank took a lap around my condo before settling on Tate's shoulder, something that I was shocked to see. Perhaps the bird could sense his unhappy spirit. Or perhaps he was just a grape trollop. Whatever the case Tate sat on the sofa, feeding Frank treats as I threw together a quick dinner for the two of us. Our phones were off for the night to give Tate some respite. After a light meal of beef strips over wild rice, salad, and sparkling water, we put Frank to bed.

"Does he always curse at you when you put him to bed?" Tate asked.

"Mm, yes, the cursing is my fault. You take the bedroom. I will go sleep in my guest room."

Tate paused by the large crate that now was covered with a sheet. His gaze found mine. "Why are you sleeping in another room?"

"I thought you should rest without me rutting against you. I seem to have a weakness for you and cannot keep my hands to myself."

He smiled. It was the first smile that I'd seen on him since this latest mess had blown up. "I like you rutting on me."

With that knowledge, I led him to my bed, stripped him of every last stitch of clothing, and gathered him close to me. Somehow I managed to keep my cock to myself, and Tate slept fitfully curled into my side. Whatever came at us next I felt that we'd grown closer today and could handle anything fate threw at us.

FATE WAS A MISERABLE COW-FACED, TRINKET-LOVING whore.

Our first game back from that tumultuous Canadian road trip was against the Harrisburg Railers. I had great respect for the Railers. They'd been one of the top teams in the league for a few years, solid, cohesive, and incredibly inclusive. Everything that I hoped to see the Raptors become. I was good friends with Stan; he and I were part of a Russian group on Facebook and often spoke online about life in America.

Also, I enjoyed playing them. They never slacked off or played a B-game even though we were not quite at the same level they were. Yet. Trying to defend against Tennant Rowe-Madsen was challenging and invigorating. Or used to be. Tonight the man was working under my skin like a rotted sliver.

Andre had been relegated to sitting on the bench, and Colorado was in net. Tate and Tennant had spent a long time chatting before we had changed, then during warm-up, and even now when they were on the ice at the same time they were talking. And smiling. And laughing at jokes that they didn't share with the others. Others like me. By the second period the friendly banter between the two was making my teeth grate. Rowe-Madsen took advantage of my irritation with his pretty face. He was fast and agile. Trying to catch him was like trying to capture mercury with chopsticks. Tonight, he was extra flashy, extra smiley, extra pretty, and Tate was enraptured, I was sure of it. So, I got stupid and checked Rowe into my own goalie by mistake. Well the check wasn't a mistake. That was on purpose, but him flying into Penn and knocking him off his skates wasn't intended.

As soon as I hit him I knew that I'd made a mistake, and I knew exactly what it was I was feeling. None of my trouble was with Tennant. It was with me. I was feeling jealous. It was a foreign emotion to me, as I had high self-confidence. Mulling over why I was being such a fucking jerk, I planted my ass on the bench, let Coach yell at the back of my head because the shouting was deserved, and then glanced down the line to find Tate staring at me.

A silent sort of thing passed between us. What it was I

would have been hard pressed to explain, but I saw many things in his warm brown eyes. He chewed on his mouthguard and raised one eyebrow. I shrugged. He rolled his eyes. I closed my eyes and inclined my head to ask for forgiveness. Coach was still yelling, the fans were still jeering the Railers, and the moron behind us was still holding that miserable sign about Tate being the biggest turd on the SHT line against the glass. None of that mattered though. I opened my eyes and saw Tate tap his visor as if to say all was forgiven. Or I read it that way. Perhaps he was using some sort of Texas sign language to tell me to fuck off. I'd not know for sure until after the game, when we were all meeting up with Ryker, Jacob, and the Railers for a late meal at one of our famous Mexican restaurants. Perhaps Tate would want to go back to his place after the meal. Perhaps he was done with my stupid old jealous pushy ass. Perhaps I needed to apologize to Tennant and Colorado and Coach as well. I sighed and spit on the floor. This being in a relationship with my teammate was causing just as much havoc as I knew it would. Yet I was in no hurry to not wake up with Tate's long, strong body next to mine.

WE LOST TO THE RAILERS BUT ONLY JUST AND IN overtime. Which pushed back our Mexican meal, which meant that Tate and I were in the parking lot behind the eatery at three in the morning, pinkie fingers hooked, looking at each other under a black velvet Arizona sky.

"I should go home," he said, but his eyes told a different story.

"You should come to my home. Frank will want his grapes."

"And you? What would you want from me?"

"All that you're willing to give me, *zvedya moya.*"

He grew bold then, leaning in to steal a kiss.

"About damn time you two came out," Eli's voice rang out, startling us apart. My partner on the ice sauntered up to us, his face a smug mask. "We have a pool."

"We're not out, we're not— a pool?" I asked, keeping my pinkie finger linked with Tate's.

"Oh yeah, it's been running for a couple of weeks now. A Where-Will-Sugar-and-Ice-be-Caught-Sucking-Face?' pool. I think I might have just won!"

"There is no winning. We are not out, and as my friend I ask you to keep what you have seen to yourself. Our lives are too complicated for a romance to burst into the limelight."

"But there must be five hundred bucks in the till. Ryker had you two down to be caught in the showers, which I knew was far too forward for the Iceberg. Alex said you'd be caught in the skate room. Again, too forward. Penn said you'd be caught in the sin bin which I think is some pansexual fantasy of his or something, but yeah, so not Vlad. Henry guessed you'd be seen smooching by the concession stands, also not Vlad. But, I had a parking lot behind a Mexican restaurant after a meal with the Railers."

"Fuck you. You're feeding me bullshit," I snapped.

Tate sniggered, then slid an arm around my waist. My eyes flared. Eli clapped my shoulder.

"Yeah, I'm fucking with you. Be nice to this old shit, okay, Sugar?"

"I'll be nice to him, I promise," Tate replied as Eli slipped around us.

"Good, I'd hate to have to kick your ass. Oh, and by the way? There really *is* a pool and I just won." Eli shouted, then dashed to catch his ride home with Henry and Apollo.

"If I find out there is a pool…"

Tate pulled me to my car. "Forget about the pool. Let's go home. Your home. Your bed."

That I was more than happy to do.

I *would* find out about the pool though…

Chapter Eleven

Tate

THE CAR RIDE BACK TO MY PLACE THE NEXT MORNING WAS quiet.

I'd stayed overnight with Vlad, yes, I'd fed Frank grapes, and yes, I'd felt quieter and chilled and protected. But out here on a fresh day heading home I still had the mess in my head that wouldn't go away.

It had started with a blurry photo tweeted a few hours back that pictured me leaving the station, and another with Vlad there, and I couldn't even begin to read some of the comments below it, but the Internet was quick to judge. I saw words like *millionaires get away with hurting people*, and worse, and I wasn't ready to face any of that.

Vlad had been quiet since the text, withdrawn. He didn't hug me and tell me it was okay; in fact he was pissed, and I couldn't help but feel that some of that was directed at me.

Then there was the elephant in the room we both ignored.

There were two elephants in fact, but Lacey was the obvious one, sitting there waiting to be dealt with. Only, I was so done with talking about her and defending myself, and somehow last night I'd managed to stuff her in a teeny tiny box and hide her on a dusty shelf somewhere in the back of my mind, and thankfully Vlad hadn't mentioned her once.

I hadn't been arrested, hell there was nothing to charge me with, and the interview had gone well until the moment the cop had slid over the bank statement that showed the million dollar deposit to Lacey's investment account. I hadn't even told Vlad about that fuck up yet, and the ramifications for the team as a whole.

The detective had suggested with a sly tone that giving Lacey money made it look as if I was paying her off. My lawyer, or rather, the team lawyer, had told him to go fuck himself. Not in quite those terms, but with lots of legal talk that confused me, but had the detective nodding.

Ten said I needed to talk to some guy called Layton Foxx, the marketing social fixes-everything guy from the Railers, gave me his number, and said that there wasn't much the man couldn't fix. Not only to deal with the Lacey issue, but also to help with the star goalie and his damn emu. *He can even fix stupid*, Tennant had said, *We have an* Adler, *and Layton fixed him.*

Maybe I would take up the offer for the Lacey issue, but Vlad struck me as the kind of man who was very much not interested in help, with or without emus. He was control personified.

I had to wonder though, after yesterday and the hand-holding on the plane, and Eli's stupid joke about the pool, was Vlad feeling like maybe his grip on everything was slipping away?

Is this my fault?

I couldn't imagine the worries and fears in his head about what would happen back home if everything came out. Dwight had suggested a meeting, a restraining order, a public statement, in his official lawyer-type way. I didn't want that, especially if it meant Vlad got pulled into the mess. All I wanted to do was play hockey.

Then, there was the other elephant, Tennant Rowe. Last night we'd gone back to Vlad's, had sex that was less about getting off and more about care, then hugging, and not once had we mentioned Ten's name. Only this morning, after the text with the blurry photo, Ten had texted me with Layton's number, and also a message that was all about keeping positive.

It made me smile, but when I'd told Vlad about it, he'd been tight-lipped.

I'd seen the focus in his game when he'd hip-checked Ten and sent him careening into Colorado, and I'd have to have been an idiot not to notice the way he'd looked from Ten to me when we were talking.

"Ten and I cleared the air," I announced, as we drew closer to my house. There was little traffic and we had maybe five minutes in the car before he dropped me there so I could drive separately to the arena. Maybe I shouldn't have mentioned Ten; with hindsight, possibly it was a bad idea? "That was what the text was about, just laughing is all."

Why am I defending myself?

"Good," he murmured, but it was too low for me to make out if he was lying.

"We laughed that I had a crush on him."

Vlad sent me a sharp glare. "Rowe laughed at you?"

"No, we laughed together. He said, if only he'd known, then—"

"What?" Vlad barked. "What would he have done? Would you have chosen him over Lacey? What *would* you have done?"

I blinked at Vlad as he turned into my drive and entered the code for the gate. There were a few reporters clustered there, but Vlad ignored them, and so did I. Tinted windows were my saving grace, and he stopped the car just inside the gate watching for it to shut, likely checking no paparazzi got in to take photos. It hit me that the fact Vlad taking me home might look bad.

"Maybe you shouldn't have driven me home, if they realize it's your car—"

"I am captain bring home teammate," he snapped, his Russian showing big time. "Tell me about Ten."

"Huh?"

"Madsen-Rowe. You started, that if only he'd known…"

"Oh, well, he admitted he would have understood the reasons why I couldn't properly look him in the face," I finished. "And how he had this perpetual feeling that he'd made me angry about something. He said he always felt like number two at Dallas, and would never be first line, and he thanked me for it, said going to the Railers was the best thing that happened to him. I don't think he realized that I pushed to be number one just to impress him."

Vlad muttered something in a low voice, Russian; I couldn't understand any of it.

He killed the engine, and turned in his seat.

"You are better than Tennant *Rainbow Gay* Madsen-Rowe." He was utterly focused on me and I don't know what he expected me to say.

"Jeez Vlad, given that you and I are... that you... fuck, that was insulting to Ten," I finally managed to force out.

"Given that you and I are what?" he asked as if the answer didn't matter at all.

I shriveled a little inside. "Tog—Sleeping together."

Vlad huffed. "Tennant had his hands on you."

What the hell was happening here? "He was telling me about this Layton guy who could help you with the emu situation—"

"I do not want help—"

"Maybe you need—"

"I need no one who thinks they can come into my life and tell me what to do. What about you? Do you want to tell me what to do, when you can't even fix your own life?"

I stared at him and wondered exactly what the hell we were doing.

"Vlad, what are we even arguing about?"

He scowled. "Tennant—"

"That's not it."

"Colorado and his fucking emu will drive me insane—"

"That's not it either. What is going on here? Are you trying to start an argument?"

He softened for a moment. "No."

"Are you scared of something?" I asked, and wondered if I was more perceptive than I'd thought when that steely Russian gaze reappeared and his pale eyes were chips of ice.

"I will see you at the arena," he said.

"Vlad—"

"At the arena," he repeated, and this time he faced forward.

I was out of the car faster that Usain Bolt out of his blocks, and into my house with just as much speed and I never once glanced back at Vlad in his big-ass SUV, or as the gates opened, or even as they shut. I was inside my house, and fuck the big Russian for wanting to start an argument, because if he wanted to stop what we were doing then he needed to say it, not force me away with his misery and ice.

I showered, cursed a lot, stomped around my place, ignored three calls from the team lawyer, and one from Sam. The only one I answered was from Henry, who was *just checking in.* When I'd reassured him that everything was fine, and then the cell vibrated with a text from Ryker, I turned the damn thing off. I was done with the well wishes, the concern, and most of all I was done with the frustrating Russian who'd dumped me at my place and tried to make us argue.

Getting to the arena for practice was easy enough, despite the traffic. One thing about having tinted windows was that I could look out but no one would see it was me.

People in other cars sang along to music, they were chatting, animated. I bet none of them had a psycho ex leveling accusations that they'd hurt her, or a sort-of-lover who wanted to start a fight with me for god knows what purpose. I had a memory of a moment, a flashback from when I was a kid, when I knew I was heading home to face the consequences of something I'd done. Maybe it had been a school prank, or low marks on my reports, but I would look into windows of houses we passed, and wonder if I could swap places with some other kid. One who *wasn't* in trouble.

I pulled up alongside a van, a kid staring out at the passing cars, Raptors stickers in the windows. He was wearing a Raptors hoodie, and it hit me. I wondered how many people in cars here would see me and want to change places with me? Wannabe NHL'ers, kids who were desperate to play? We were at least two stops back from the lights, and in a moment of love and peace and kindness, I lowered my window, and the kid staring out from his car caught the movement, then rubbernecked, and then shouted my name before he lowered his window.

"TATE!" he called, and I saw his mom look over her shoulder and then over at me. She appeared to have control over the back windows and it began to raise, as she mouthed *sorry* at me. I shook my head, made the universal sign for lowering the window and then reached into the back of my car where I knew for sure I had a stack of jerseys. I held one up, but the light changed and we all had to shuffle forward. I really hoped the kid who'd shouted my name stopped next to me again, and I was so damned pleased when he did. The mom shrugged in a what-can-you-do kind of manner and the kid lowered his window all the way. We were no more than six feet apart.

"Hi," I called over. "What's your name?"

"Lucas Bowyer, I play hockey for the mini-slide-Eagles."

"What position?"

"Center, just like you." He was so animated it was infectious. This was why I played, this childish excitement was still inside me every time I hit the ice.

"Would you like a jersey?" I called over.

"YES!" he shouted, and then with prompting from his mom he added a belated "Please." I tossed him a jersey, then another where I'd scribbled my name next to my number, rooted around, found a couple of pucks, and then emptied a Raptors gym bag and tossed all of that to him as well.

"Do you come to the games?"

He wrinkled his nose at that. "Once," he murmured.

I could fix that. Tickets weren't cheap, even to see the Raptors, but I got freebies for every game. "Mrs. Bowyer?" I called. "Go to Will-Call and you tell them that Tate sent you, I'll leave your son's name, maybe you can get tickets for when we play Ottawa tomorrow?"

She smiled at me, nodded, but then the traffic moved and, after exchanging virtual high fives with Lucas, I headed on to the arena. I needed to get back to my visits to the hospital, I hadn't been in a couple of weeks, and I hoped to hell I could sneak in and not have the whole Lacey shit causing me issues.

Decision made, I arrived at the arena with a huge grin

on my face. I was Tate Collins, I was a hockey player, and no one could take that away from me.

Only the team lawyer, Dwight not-so-perky Perkins, was waiting for me, standing with one of the team owners, Mark, and I wished there was another way into the arena because the last thing I wanted to do was harsh the buzz I had going. But neither of them appeared to be pissed, or as if they had something to say to me that was going to change the direction of my life.

"A word?" Mark said, and opened the door to what looked like a janitor's room, and then closing it behind the three of us. I can honestly say I've never had a meeting in a room that smelled of bleach and contained at least six mops.

"What's happened?" I asked, because this was so unreal.

"We wanted to cross the Ts," Dwight began.

"There are no charges," Mark continued. "You ex has released this." He thrust a phone at me, and I scrolled down the Twitter thread. "She admits that you're a good guy, and that comments were taken out of context. She's also mentioned that she's seeking help for her mental health." The post had seven thousand likes already, and it had only been posted two hours ago, right when I was arguing with Vlad. She'd played it to perfection, hundreds of thousands of likes of her losing her shit over me, and there would be just as many of her saying her pointed comments were taken out of context, with sympathy for her admission she looking for help. She was working this angle hard and I was caught in the crossfire.

"The million dollars," Mark said, in that quiet tone

of his.

"I shouldn't have done that, but it wasn't for the reason you think."

"What was the reason?"

The last thing I wanted to do was go into details. "Do I have to say?"

Mark shook his head "Probably best not to. Dwight has non-disclosure paperwork for her to sign. The Raptors want this done."

"I want this done," I agreed.

"Okay." Mark held out his hand to shake. "Meeting adjourned." He opened the door and the three of us stepped out, just as Colorado passed. He frowned, looked at me, then Mark, and then at poor Dwight.

"Dwight, dude, did you just come out of the closet?"

"No, I—"

Colorado ignored him. "Welcome to the rainbow, my man!" he said and enthusiastically pumped Dwight's hand, before leaving and cackling.

Hell, at least there was no emu trailing him, or a single sign of a groupie. That was one thing I suppose. I stopped off at Will-Call, because I wanted to keep a promise I'd made, added the name Lucas Bowyer to the list, plus three others, and said it was good for any game, then I jogged to the locker room, now just under five minutes from practice time.

VLAD WAS ALREADY IN THE LOCKER ROOM, SUITED UP, head bent, tying his laces, murmuring to himself in Russian as he always did when he was lacing. Probably blessing the skates, or something. Henry was also here, but he was pacing, and only stopped when he caught sight of me. The tension in him eased in an instant.

"Thought you might not be here," he said, and a couple of the other guys glanced up and nodded at me. Last they'd heard I was taken in for questioning, and this was the point where the team either believed me without reservation or I explained the situation.

"It's all bullshit," Ryker began.

"Total fucking bullshit," Colorado elaborated.

I heard a few more guys say the same thing, agreeing, supporting me.

"She's fully retracted the statement," I said during a lull in the conversation, and got a succession of high fives, and a bro-hug from Henry.

"What are we? Fisherwomen?" Vlad snapped. "Gossiping like children. Ice, now."

I wasn't even kitted up. Hell, I hadn't even opened my bag, and he glared at me. "Collins, get your ass changed and out on the ice."

I exchanged glances with Coach Carmichael, who sent me a look of confusion, but as the guys left, and Vlad was last, I said in my loudest clearest voice to Coach.

"Our captain must have got out of the wrong side of bed."

Coach raised an eyebrow, I concentrated on getting into my gear, taping, and lacing, and Coach thrust a gray jersey at me. I'd be playing with my line, against the JAR line, and when I spotted Vlad's white jersey, I thought that today, the shit was going to hit the fan.

The first time he locked me in the corner, his body

weight pinning mine, I used my ass, and the muscles in my legs to heave him off, shuffled the puck between his legs, hefted it to Sam who shot on Andre, and the gray team had the first goal of the practice session.

The second time he had me in the corner he'd learned to steady himself to the point he was immoveable. So I went limp, loosened every muscle, and he fell forward, and again I shuttled the puck, this time to Henry, who did this awesome tape-to-tape pass to Sam, who then passed it back, and Henry got the gray team's second goal.

Meanwhile I was floundering in the corner, stuck under a fallen Vlad, who rolled free. Thank fuck it was Eli, Vlad's D-partner, who focused on me next, but he was easy to get away from, only of course that left Vlad to intercept my pass, and it was the white team who got the next shot, although we had Colorado in net and he swatted it away like he would a fly.

We switched to line changes, moved some things around, and the two hours seemed to rush by. Through every moment of it Vlad wasn't the consummate professional where nothing touched him. He was edgy and crabby, and wouldn't meet my eye, and temper snapped in his icy eyes. It wasn't only me that noticed the change in him today.

"What crawled up Vlad's ass and died?" Ryker faux-whispered to Sam.

"Maybe his parrot is ill," Sam suggested with a shrug.

"Frank is fine," I defended, and Sam sent me a look that spoke volumes.

"So he's just in a mood for no reason," Sam pushed.

"You're up!" Coach called, and when no one else

moved, I assumed it was me. "I want to see you get past Vlad to Colorado, work the edges."

I got past him easily; he wasn't even fucking trying.

"Stop me," I snapped at him, and he skated backward and into position, this time fighting more, but I had him on the ropes, and if Colorado had been a shit goalie I would have gotten another goal.

I faced up to Vlad, caught his gaze, stared at him hard, daring him to fight. I was pissed now. I didn't care what he thought was happening with us fucking, but messing with the game, that wasn't on. I shoved him with my stick, caught him off guard, and he stumbled. The puck was on the ice between us and I shoved him again, and again, and each time he pressed back harder, until at last we had a battle to get the puck, and this time I had to work every muscle to get past him. With a last ditch poke of his stick he saved the puck and iced it to the other end where the team stood in clusters.

We were face-to-face, him staring at me impassively.

"Fuck you," I said, although I kept it low enough so only he would hear. "Don't you dare do this shit with me, okay?" I was defying him, telling him how angry I was, and there was nothing in his expression.

"Maybe you should stop staring at Tennant Madsen-Rowe then," he bit out with unleashed fury, and then I could see him shut down, the temper subside, the control come back with a vengeance. Then he stared back at me, and god, I wanted to shove him again.

"What?" I honestly wasn't sure I heard right.

"I won't be second choice when I have so much to lose," he murmured, as if it meant nothing to him that he was breaking my heart in the middle of the rink. He brushed past me and headed for Colorado who fist-bumped him and then, heads together, they chatted. What was Vlad saying to Colorado? Was it about us? I thought we were on the down-low?

Were being the operative word.

I skated back to Alex who stick-tapped my shin.

"Nice battle."

I heard a couple of the other skaters wondering about what the hell was going on with their captain, and all I could feel was anger, misery, and guilt. It took me showering, then dressing, before I calmed down.

"Coffee?" Ryker asked.

"I'm okay—"

"Coffee," he repeated, and I realized belatedly that this was some of messed-up intervention when Henry, Alex and Sam walked up to stand by me as well.

I gave in and we headed for The Coffee Bean, a local place with hidden corners and a ton of discretion, and I thought of anything to talk about that wasn't Vlad, inevitably leading to the kid I'd met this morning.

"It was so cool, he was a huge hockey fan, says his favorite is Ryker."

Ryker buffed his nails on his T-shirt. "Kid has good taste."

Alex shoved at him. "Whatever, dude."

"He plays as well."

"Cool, we should go see his team, give them a few jerseys with a decent name on it," Ryker teased, which this time earned a kick from me, under the table. At least Ryker was interested in knowing more and there was something intriguing about Lucas with his bright blue eyes and his excitement for hockey. "We do all kinds of outreach with kids' teams here."

"Yeah, we used to do that in Dallas."

"This isn't Dallas," they all chorused, and then sniggered as if it was the funniest joke on the planet. I couldn't help smiling, but shook my head as if it was too stupid to rise to it.

"Which team does he play for?" Alex asked

I couldn't recall at first, "Something with slide in it?"

Ryker exchanged a look with Henry. "Mini-slide-Eagles maybe?"

"That's it."

"That's a sled team," he said, and smiled broadly, "such a good bunch of kids, all with their own issues, most of them unable to walk or with other disabilities but all hooked on hockey, I know that Coach Carmichael does some work with them."

I didn't know how to feel. The words sled hockey conjured up so many images, of bravery, and excitement, and finding new ways to play hockey. Was I sad that Lucas was maybe sick? Or unable to walk or—

"Stop thinking about the bad shit and come and see it for real," Ryker murmured. "I'm up for a visit with Coach, getting involved, wanna come with me?"

I thought about my visits to the cancer ward, the ones no one knew about, where I tried my best to be what they needed me to be. But I had more time; in fact, outside of hockey I had all the time in the freaking world.

And right now, this sounded like exactly what I needed to do.

Chapter Twelve

Vlad

IT SEEMED AS IF THE ROWE-MADSEN MEN WERE determined to poke this grumpy bruin.

After my nonsense with Tate, and yes I knew it had been nonsense but yet it had bubbled out of me like pus from a gangrenous wound, I'd planned on distancing myself from Tate for a few days, or at least a few hours. My life was out of control. *I* was out of control. Anxiety gnawed at me as I made my way out of the barn, eager to go home, sit and think, plan, plot, and try to find a path back to my once orderly life. Instead Ryker Madsen cornered me as I was leaving and snared me with the one thing that I could never say '*Nyet*' to—children in need.

I, of course, had many charities in Tucson that I donated my time and money to, as we all did. Penn spent a goodly amount of his free time helping to raise funds for the local domestic abuse shelter, one of the few responsible things he seemed capable of doing. I helped raise funds for cancer victims in memory of my cousin who had died at eighteen from that terrible disease. I'd even had my agent set up a fund to help children who survived cancer go onto college by paying tuition for one child per year. I donated to animal rescues, and several bird rescue and avian sanctuaries in the state. Back home, I sponsored youth hockey teams and sent money to orphanages. Still, this sled hockey team was not one that I was familiar with, but if they needed help, I would be there. My tangled feelings for Tate would be pushed aside. Or so I thought.

But I'd been played for an idiot. Because Tate was right there and I couldn't back out now. One word from a child getting excited as I arrived was more than enough to have me stay.

During the next two hours, my head became more chaotic as I watched Tate interact with the children on the mini-sled team. I'd heard of sled hockey, of course, and had even written a few checks to the Tucson league, but this was my first hands-on experience. It was beyond moving to see all the children, and adults, with disabilities hitting the ice. And Tate...

Well, Tate was incredible with children. His genuine goodness and warmth drew the children to him, as well as the adults involved in the league. I found my gaze moving to him time and again, his smile stirring up the mess of confusion in my heart and head. Finally, after a photo-op with the director of the league, Jonas McKenzie, a strikingly handsome ex-Army captain who'd lost a leg serving his country in a faraway desert, I managed to break free. Ryker and Tate stayed behind to talk with Jonas. I needed distance.

Once I was home, and Frank was seated on the windowsill calling *"Suka! Suka! Suka!"* at my neighbor as he washed his car, I pulled up Facebook, hoping to get lost in the mundane mindlessness of social media and funny parrot videos.

"Frank, come have a grape," I called in Russian. It was a blessing that no one in my community spoke my native tongue. I was sure Phil next door would not appreciate being called a bitch for hours on end. The bird ignored me, happier being crude at the moment, it seemed. There were no funny parrot videos to watch, so I visited the Russian chat group the NHL players had.

I was pleased to see that Stan Lyamin was online and talking about socks with holes in the toes and a puppet he was trying to make for his youngest son. I smiled at the discussion, keeping mostly to myself, and wondering how it was that Stan had managed a marriage with one of his teammates. True, he was not a team captain but he was the goalie, which was just as important a role in the locker room dynamics of a team. Had he and Eric had troubles with loving and playing together? Or was it me making the problems? He too had family back home to be concerned about, or so I thought.

I sent him a private message and we were soon talking to each other with no other loudmouthed Russians interfering.

"Zdravstvuy, drug moy," I opened with once we'd moved into our own space.

"Hello, my friend back for you. Please, we must speak

in English for my glowing improvements in the language is making big hits," Stan replied, holding his phone upward so that I was looking down at him. "Is making good selfie position for to talk. My neck is making like a turkey my children say."

"Your neck is not a turkey at all," I replied, pushing to my feet to go to the kitchen. I passed Frank tormenting my neighbor through the screen.

"Your bird has big bad mouth!" Stan roared at the filth coming from Frank.

"Yes, I have given him a wide vocabulary of dirty words," I tossed out, trying to ignore the cussing as I padded to the fridge for a bottle of water. "I wished to speak to you of private matters. Are you childless at the moment?"

"Yes, I am home alone like that movie with the two bandits who get paint cans in the forehead."

"Ah, good." I had no idea what movie he was speaking of. I pulled out a bottle of lemon-lime sparkling water, shut the fridge, and sat at the island. Perhaps I needed to watch more mainstream movies. Maybe if I did things that others did—like watch silly movies—I'd not feel so left out and upset about Tennant Rowe. Which was stupid. Tate and Tennant were friends, that was all. Yes, he had been attracted to him, but now he was my lover and I was sure he was well pleased. Wasn't he?

"Vlad, do you wish to speak soon or should I go make a sock puppet as you stare at water bottle?"

My attention snapped back to my phone resting on the countertop. "Sorry, I am…there is this thing that I am wrestling with. A...sort of attraction to someone on my team."

Stan's gray eyes flared. He glanced at the sock on his hand, then back at me. "I did not know you were gay."

"Mm, well, it has been a secret. My family back home..."

"Ah yes, I know that worry well. Say nothing more. So, you are mad worried over the press people finding out and the news going back to Russia?"

"Yes, that, and the..." I glanced from the phone to the bird in the window. "I have...forever I have always been in control of my life. What was said about me, what I projected, what I let the world know, what men I had relations with. Then Tate..."

"Ah yes, *then Tate*. I understand. Mine was "then Eric" although Eric and I had known each other previously but still when he came to Harrisburg things went flopsy and mopsy for a bit."

"How do you do it? How do you play with a man you're in love with?"

A moment went by as I listened to that word bouncing around my kitchen like a fly trying madly to find an open door. *Love.*

"You find way. If you love him, then you find way. Is simple, no?"

"No, it is not simple. It is complex."

"Only because you make it confused. Love is not complex; we people make it so. Love is easy and freeing once you stop seeking to control it. We humans cannot control love. We must just ride along on it, hands in the air, like big roller coaster ride with many shouts of joy and tears of upset. Maybe you need to let go of the bar and throw your hands in the air?"

I sat back in my stool, gaping at the man with the warm gray eyes and his hand inside an old sock. Let go of the bar. That was simple to say. I had held the bar tightly my whole life. What if I let go and fell out, plummeting to my death as Tate rode another ride. Like that tilting whirly thing. Tate seemed a tilting whirly sort.

"Vlad, you are staring Superman holes in water bottle again," Stan said, pulling me from the amusement park setting up inside my head.

"I am sorry. My mind is tangled. You have given me much to think on." I paused, still lost in thought. "Tell me of how you managed things back home. Is your family safe? Has your marriage come back to harm them? I fear that if I am forthcoming with my sexuality that it will hurt my loved ones."

Stan sighed as if he carried the weight of the world on his wide shoulders. "Yes, it is a concern that makes me heavy sad. So far there has been no large problems but I do not go back often now that Mama is here. You go back yes? Every summer?"

"Yes."

"Mm, then perhaps you will face more hostility. I cannot tell you which path is less rocky road. Each man must choose his own way, but I do know that I could not imagine my life without my husband and my children. Please, my friend, be mindful of caution. Is there a way to bring your family over here?"

"No, I do not think so. My brother Dimi, you know him, he plays for the KHL and is soon to be engaged to a lovely girl. My parents…I cannot see them leaving their home for America." My head was beginning to ache a bit, as it always did when I tried to juggle who I was with where I came from.

"Ah well, then you will have to be making a walk on a tight rope. Do you love Tate deeply?"

"I…my feelings are deep, yes," I confessed.

"Then it is a hard pick to make, not like picking nose which is easy. Please, if you wish more talking time, call me. I will send you my cell phone number. I am always loving to talk my Russian brothers."

"Thank you, Stan. I will let you go now. Finish your puppet before the children come back home."

"Do you wish more help on love and marriage and family? I can show you how to make puppets from old socks. I have buttons and ribbons!"

"No, I am…I do not need puppets. But thank you for taking time to speak with me. You are a good friend. Give your family and husband my love. They are lucky to have you."

"Please to let me know how things with Tate go?" The puppet was speaking now. I shook my head, chuckled at the sock pressed up to the camera, called Stan a foolish ass, and we said our goodbyes.

Long after the phone call ended I sat in the kitchen, staring at my untouched bottle of water, thinking. Frank flew in to join me. Landing on the island, he began mouthing the cap on my water bottle. I reached out to stroke him. He lowered his head to allow me to rub his neck, petting against the lie of the feathers which was opposite of how one would pet a dog. He loved to be scratched behind his ears, and so I sat there stroking him as I mulled over Stan's wise words. Perhaps, just perhaps, I did need to throw my hands into the air. Just this once...

I glanced at Frank. He gave my hand a kiss, opening his beak and touching his tongue to my finger. I smiled at him, called him to my hand, and carried him to his crate. He was happy to settle into his pen, as his feed dishes were full. As he feasted on fruity-flavored pellets, I went back to the kitchen, found my phone, and sent Tate a text.

I want to ride with you. Please, come to me so we can talk. – V

It seemed to take forever for him to reply but it was perhaps thirty minutes or so.

Sorry, phone died. Got a charge from Ryker fast to reply. Ride what? Where and when to talk? – T

My place. Soon as possible. Please. -V

Be there in thirty. <3 -T

HE ARRIVED IN TWENTY. IT WAS FAR TOO LONG AND FAR too short.

I let him in and he went right to Frank, who showed off, called Tate a fucker in Russian and then asked for a grape. Tate looked over his shoulder at me, seeking permission to feed the bird. I nodded and went off to find some grapes in the fridge. Plucking a bunch free, I then walked back to the cage, planting myself beside Tate. He smelled fresh and citrusy. I yearned to pick him up, carry him to my bed, and lose myself in him.

"You said something about a ride with me?" he said as he pulled a fat red grape from the stem and held it between the wires of the cage. Frank hustled over on his perch, wings out, head bobbing, and took the grape with a cry of joy.

"Yes, I want to ride with you. On the rollercoaster of love."

"Is that like the freeway of love?"

"I get that joke," I said and he gave me a nudge of his elbow. "It was a song, I know songs, movies not so much."

He gave the parrot another grape, his jaw firming up a bit. Then he turned to look at me, really look at me, into me, boring deep.

"There's nothing between me and Tennant, it was just a stupid crush. I wish it had never come out, I should have never told anyone but I thought…well, what I think about her isn't important to talk about now. Now I want to talk about us. Are you saying you want to date me? Come out? Be seen together in public? Make a statement? Forgive me being dense but I'm all sorts of fucked up at the moment."

"Fucked up! Fucked up!" Frank squawked and clicked his beak.

Tate grimaced. "Oh man, I'm sorry. I didn't think he would pick that up."

"It's fine," I said, my gaze roaming over his face, settling on his mouth and how pink and full his lower lip was. "He says worse. I know that Tennant is not your man, I am, yes?"

"Yeah, if you want to be." He tossed a grape into his mouth, trying to be nonchalant but the tension was obvious in the set of his shoulders. I placed a hand to his neck, rubbing at the tense muscles.

"I would like to be very much. But we cannot be out. We must be discreet, for the safety of others, not for me. If it were for me I would announce our romance to the world." A winsome smile lifted his lips. "I would lay you down and feed you grapes and cover your flesh with kisses."

The tender smile blossomed into something sinful. He slid his hand into mine and pulled me to my bedroom, moving around me when we were near the bed.

"Do it." He handed me the grapes, the stem warmed from being between his fingers. "Do it all. Lay me down, feed me grapes, cover my flesh with kisses."

"Are you sure you want to continue this with me? You could be with another man or woman who would be out with you, living without secrets."

"I'm sure. Now stop dawdling and feed me grapes."

I cupped a hand around his neck, then led his mouth to mine. His lips were sweeter than any fruit on the planet. As was his body, which I bared slowly, peeling his clothes from him much as one would the delicate skin of a grape. I kissed his brow, then slipped a grape between his lips. Then I kissed his nose and fed him another grape. Then I tasted his lips, his chin, his throat, his chest, his tight nipples, each point of adoration followed by a taste of grape. His movements were brash, aggressive, lusty as I stretched out the lovemaking, teasing and tasting, licking a hot path down the inside of his thigh, worshipping his ankle and the arch of his foot before nibbling my way back upward, suckling on his balls until he cried out in frustration, then made the same languid path up and down the other leg.

"We have a few grapes left," I stated as I nuzzled his sac, lifting it out of the way so I could tongue the space between his nuts and his tight hole.

"Oh for fuck…forget the grapes. I'm…ahhh, shit Vlad, yes, do that again." He purred like a cat with cream. I placed my hands on his thighs and pushed them wider, angling my shoulders between his powerful legs. Tempted beyond rational thought, I longed to take one of those round fruits and insert it into him, then fish it out with my tongue. Instead I used a finger, slippery with spit, and began working him open as I sucked on his balls. His cock was stiff, the head plum-colored and slick with pre-cum. "I'm going to suck on the head of your cock. Look at it, look how red it is, how wet, how it yearns to be in my mouth. Watch me sucking you while I stretch your ass."

Brown eyes hot with lust settled on me, his lips parted, his tongue between his white teeth. He hissed and spasmed when I pulled just the head of him between my lips. My finger went deeper, another joined it, and then a third as I swirled my tongue around his cockhead. His fingers dug into the bedding, pulling the sheets upward into mounds. A burst of pre-cum hit my mouth so I pulled off and out, lapping my way up his body, stopping only to tug at his nipples. He was frantic beneath me, clawing at the bed or at my back, his strong legs tilting his ass up from the mattress, his mouth moving over my arms, biting gently on my shoulder as I settled over him.

"Do you like my cock in your ass, *Zvedva moya?*"

"Love it…give it to me now, please?"

"So pushy. Have you forgotten who is in charge?"

He shook his head, his lips too tempting to not crush with mine. His tongue met mine, parried and danced with it. I slid my arms around him and threw my weight to the side, rolling us over with a grunt. The kiss broke. He settled on my thighs, his cock resting on my belly, mine nestled between those tasty round orbs of his.

"I know who's in charge," he replied breathlessly, moving his hips back and forth, rubbing his cock over me as my prick slipped over up and down the crack of his ass. For a man who had never been with another man before, he was a natural cock tease.

"Tonight you are, my star. Tonight, I throw my arms up and let you lead. Tonight, I give myself to you, all of me," I whispered, reaching over my head to wrap my fingers around the posts of my headboard. His eyes rounded for a moment, then the passion took over, and so did he. Tate rolled the condom on me, then slicked it up, rising up with one hand on my chest to press a glob of lube into his ass. I groaned at the image. His head dropping down, his eyes closed, his mouth parted as he fingered his own hole for me. "Go slow, it will be deep. Do not hurt…fucking hell, Tate."

He impaled himself. A huff of pain escaped him. I tightened my hold on the bed, knowing that if I grasped his hips as I longed to do, I would fuck him into a coma. He eased up, the tightness around his jaw lessening as he rose, then slowly went back down.

"Plow horse…definitely a Russian plow horse," he gasped when he sat, my cock buried to the hilt inside him.

"Mm, the best things…are Russian," I replied around a moan.

Then the talking ceased. It was replaced with short bursts of growls and grunts, sighs and cries, and then the sounds of two men tumbling over the edge. Tate came on my chest and belly with just the slightest touch of my hand to his prick. He collapsed over me, convulsing around me, and I jerked as my orgasm swept over me. One hand on the headboard, the other finding his ass, I pushed my heels into the bed to get that extra inch. He whined as he lay atop me, his body shuddering as his cock pulsed jet after jet of cum between us.

"Oh my God," he whimpered as we lay there too spent to move. His lips moved tenderly up and down my shoulder, then my neck, and then skipped over my whiskery cheek to my mouth. He licked inside. I released his ass and carded my fingers through his hair, both hands, locking his lips to mine as I reveled in his taste.

"I agree," I sighed when the kissing slowed. "You must move." I patted his sweaty ass.

He slithered off me, settling on the bed like a bag of wet wheat. I gave his bare shoulder a kiss, then rolled off the bed, removing the condom and knotting it as I padded into the bathroom. I tossed the condom, washed my chest and belly, and then returned to Tate with a warm cloth. He rolled to his side, his gaze dreamy and soft. I fell right then. Totally. I'd been balancing on the cusp of loving the man fully, but seeing him like this, open and trusting, well-loved, I toppled completely. Somehow it would work. I would make it work. *We* would make it work.

"We have much to talk about," I said as I wiped at the drying spunk on his chest. He murmured something. I tossed the cloth to the floor and stretched out beside him, facing him, letting myself get lost in chocolate eyes. "Tell me one thing tonight and I will tell you something you wish to know about me. Is that fair?"

"Mm, yeah." He looked sleepy, his eyes heavy, his face restful. He threw out tremendous body heat. I liked it.

"Why did you ever propose to Lacey?"

That question wiped all that lazy, groggy afterglow from him in a hurry.

Chapter Thirteen

Tate

WHY DID I PROPOSE TO LACEY?

That was both the easiest and hardest question of my entire life. How could I explain why I'd done what I'd done without coming over as stupid, or flippant about the institution of marriage, something I held sacred. For me marriage meant forever, with family, and I was far from stupid.

Gullible maybe, too sensitive, yes, but not stupid.

Where did I start?

"Lacey was a team-mandated responsibility," I began, and then wriggled free of Vlad's hold and sat cross-legged with pillows behind me.

He copied me, propping himself up on the opposite end of the bed so we could talk. I kind of wanted him to lie down and shut his eyes to listen, but it was clear I had an avid audience.

"It was in your contract to marry her?" He was

confused, and I realized that maybe this wasn't how I needed to start the conversation.

"The Railers were getting heat, externally from some of the more bigoted fans, but they're up in PA and their fan base for the most was supportive, and you know, and I know, that they'll stay supportive all the time that the Railers keep putting the points up. The minute the team dips, you know what will happen, losses will get blamed on whatever they think is the weakest link. It could be racial, gender-specific, it could be sexuality. Dallas weren't flying the flag for equality as much as the Railers."

"Okay?"

"But Dallas was never worried about me."

Vlad ticked off on his fingers. "White, straight, brilliant player."

"Yep, all of that, I mean, Colorado is right, I'm properly apple-pie-flag-waving perfect. Until I met Tom. He was a new kid, apprentice to the support team, really cool guy and we got talking about *Star Wars,* and one thing led to another, someone saw us, and suddenly my bisexuality was an issue."

"Tom," Vlad said, with an ominous tone, and I kicked out at his foot.

"Kissing, Vlad, just kissing."

He grumbled low in his throat, and I kicked him again. "Stop with the jealous shit, this was two years gone. Tom is now very happily settled with Laura and Mike."

"Hmmm," he muttered, and then turned even more serious. "So, all this began because the Mr. Perfect Hockey image, with the hair product line and the power to sell merchandise, was in jeopardy?"

"Yeah, I guess."

He huffed and then crawled up the bed to me and kissed me. "You have the softest hair and the prettiest eyes."

I shoved him back, *after* I had gotten my fill of a hotly possessive kiss. "Stop interrupting me," I ordered.

He gave me a fake salute, which would have been funny, only he was crossing his legs again and flashing everything and I was suddenly in a hurry to forget the story and get back to the sexing. The bastard knew it as well, taking his time to settle before waving me to carry on.

"I got pulled in the office one day, just for a chat, kind of a how-you-doing type thing, but Dallas wasn't doing so well. Let's face it, we were in the middle of a rebuild year, and trading players away in bad deals. Management had lost control and left me and some of the remaining guys exposed. They looked to me as the skater to get the focus back on the playing and not on the bad deals, or the fact that my salary was one of the reasons we were up at cap space."

"So they made you date Lacey?"

"No. That wasn't why I dated her. I liked her, met her at a random pizza night with the team, she's actually the half-sister of Marco Ruiz, winger, third line."

"I know who Marco Ruiz is," he muttered. "Pain in my ass pushy asshole forward, likes to shove his stick where it shouldn't go."

"Yep, that's Marco, scrappy player, good guy, and we used to be friends. He introduced Lacey, we got talking, she seemed nice, we fooled around a bit, only the team thought this was the coolest thing since hockey was invented. If you listened to them, me, Tate Collins, wonder-boy, could fall in love, refocus the entire franchise, and save everything." I exaggerated my hand movements and gave my best Superman impersonation, even with arms crossed over my chest, but I could tell Vlad wasn't really getting the reference, and made a mental note to add the *Man of Steel* to my movie list for my own personal man of steel.

"Kissing this Lacey wasn't going to turn the Dallas game around, you were having a very bad year."

"Says the captain of the Craptors," I deadpanned, and he launched himself at me, tickling me into submission.

"I give! I give! Uncle!"

He stayed next to me as I continued the story and I curled into his hold, because the next part of this story wasn't so easy to tell.

"We dated a while, but she was fragile, easy to cry, and I felt as if I couldn't say anything to make her talk to someone, as if it wasn't my place. The whole thing had almost run it's course, but she…"

"What?"

"When I suggested we separate, she said she had no reason to live, I mean, what was I going to do? I could see her pain, and it wasn't just on me, I know that, but before we could even come to terms with everything, she was picked up for the hockey girlfriend show. She started saying things on camera, sharing chats that friends had shared with me in confidence, or secrets about me, stupid secrets. She would never come out with anything directly, but it was insinuated, and when the episodes aired, well the shit hit the fan in the locker room. Any trust I had in there, with all these new guys, was gone and the room was toxic, so I got an ultimatum."

"From Coach?"

"Coach? Yeah, him and the players, management, and the loss of two endorsement contracts that had once made the team look good. The message was clear, sort it out with Lacey. If I didn't love her, then I should finish it, and get it done. Move on. I knew I didn't love her, but to be so cold, that is not me." I glanced up at him, realizing I needed him to believe me, to tell me that I wasn't a bad guy.

"It's not you, it never would be."

That meant so much that I was stupidly happy, but maybe the rest of the story wouldn't make him so proud.

"So I go and see her, she's crying, and I can't stand seeing people upset, and I hug her and we start to talk about life and how I felt, and then she tells me she's pregnant."

Vlad went incredibly still, where before he'd been stroking my back, his hand didn't move and I felt him hold his breath. I was probably going to fuck things up now.

"Don't hate me," I murmured against his warm skin.

"Why would I hate you?" he choked out, but I could hear the gears in his head and I knew he had a hundred questions. "If there is a child then I will love it as yours."

My heart filled. "I proposed, immediately, call me old-fashioned but I wanted my baby to have two parents. I tried really hard, but I wasn't in love with her, but for the baby…"

"*Ya ponimayu*," he murmured, and I didn't know what it meant but it was reassuring. "I understand," he added after a short pause.

"I wanted to go to every test, because even though I didn't love her, I was convinced that one day I could make everything right. It was my baby as well. She convinced me that we should plan for the future, that she loved me, I even set up an account, put a million in, for the baby, for the future, I was so excited and I was blown away by it all. The secret made me play harder, and better, and I was carrying the team on my back just because I had this insane hope for the future."

"That was the money you sent her, for your baby."

"But there never was a baby," I whispered. "She said she'd lost it, then a few days later she admitted she'd lied…" Emotion tightened in my chest, leaving it hard to breathe.

He went back to soothing strokes on my back. "I'm so sorry."

"So the million became nothing more than a way to stop her talking. I didn't want it back, and that was our understanding. Everything fell apart, with the team, Marco had known about the baby, the non-baby, she never corrected him. He lost it and wailed on me at a practice, and then told everyone I'd been the one responsible for her losing the baby, paying her off. Jesus, I just lay there and took it all."

"Why?"

"Because Lacey… she's…" Fuck, how the hell did I explain this? "There's something about her, fragility, a sensitivity that maybe only I saw? She once told me she'd tried to take pills, to end everything. What could I do? I don't know, but we agreed, she would leave the show, keep the money, but she would get counseling. Then there was that post, about me hurting her, on her Instagram, and I don't know why she's doing it. Is it for money? For notoriety? Is it the pain that Marco feels that is making her do it? I'm furious, and sad, and overwhelmed, broken-hearted all at the same time, but I'm trying desperately to understand what she is doing."

"We need to talk to her," Vlad said.

"I'm not bullying her into—"

"Talk. Find out what is in her head. Help her if she needs it."

Shit. He'd done it. In one sentence of pure understanding and support he'd made me lose my heart, I didn't care if this relationship never stepped out of the closet, I had to tell him.

"I love you," I clung to him and he rolled us so I was sprawled across his chest. He cradled my face and I braced my arms for him to say that it was too soon, or that it was impossible, and then he smiled that beautiful smile I knew so well.

"And I love you."

THIS NEW LOVE WAS A SECRET, SOMETHING I HELD CLOSE in my heart, and I could let it out at my lowest points and know that I had Vlad in my corner. The Raptors were climbing the league, still out of the Cup race, but higher than last year. Only the last three games had been less than stellar.

Or in Colorado's words, *"this is the worst shit that has ever fucked up shit, in any shitty fucked-up arena ever"*. He was off his game, prone to stalking around looking as if he wanted to blame someone for something, and I couldn't help but think that his ire would turn on me after tonight's mess-up, one point for an overtime loss in Tampa, no points for a loss in regulation time in Carolina, and now we were a goal down against freaking Dallas in their arena, and I ached in places I didn't know could ache.

Because this was my first game back at my old team, they played a video of my highlights, the crowd had clapped, but it wasn't real, none of it was. All the players in green were respectful apart from Marco, but then he appeared to have a lot to say in my ear every time we got close.

"What is he saying?" Vlad asked me as I slid along the bench ready for my next shift.

"Same shit, different day," was all I had time to say before I got the tap to go over the boards and join a rush.

But Marco didn't stop and even though I'd promised myself that I knew the story, his constant harassment was enough to rattle me. In the locker room after the second period with only one more twenty-minute session to go I was the center of attention, and not in a good way. Coach pulled out all the typical stuff, Xs, Os and everything in between. Our D was sloppy, our forwards were making too many mistakes, we weren't playing Raptors Hockey, we needed to pull our heads out of our asses, oh and none of us were to rise to the Dallas bullshit.

He was staring right at me when he said that. I met his gaze steadily, and I saw a glimpse of disappointment when I said nothing, but I didn't have the words.

Vlad was quiet through the reaming, staring down at his skates. He didn't add anything apart from leading by example, first back onto the ice, determination in every stride.

And then it was game on.

And the gloves were off in seconds, Vlad and Marco going at it like two bulls rutting, Marco was a smaller guy but wiry and young, Vlad was a towering beast who had a point to make. I knew it was Vlad's role to get his team energized, but he wasn't going for Marco with anything other than a blazing need to take the man down. They were shouting and both fell to the ice at the same time, to be split by the officials, both in the bin with penalties, the Dallas crowd roaring their approval.

That left both teams one man down. And if there was one thing I knew well it was four-on-four hockey, and the passes between Sam, Henry and me were perfect, and in the time served we'd scored a goal and leveled the game.

Back to full strength, the fight, the goal, the hockey gods, I don't know what it was, but we played like the team we could be, winning the game in the final seconds from a lucky bounce off a Dallas stick into their own net. The hugs were relentless, but as Marco passed me he deliberately dragged his stick on my leg, enough for me to know he was there. I really needed to talk to the guy.

Coach's assessment of the game was a *hell yeah* mixed with a *that was some dumb fucking luck*. Vlad gave a small speech that built on the *hell yeah*, and then it was cool-down and showers.

By the time we were out in the hall I was exhausted, a little high on the win, worried about the conversation I knew I needed to have with Vlad over what the hell happened with Marco, and not at all looking where I was going.

"Tate?"

I knew that voice, and I stopped dead, lifting my chin and spotting Lacey sitting on a chair outside the dressing room. Some of the other guys came out behind me, but after a glance from me they left, all apart from Vlad who I knew was behind me, but who remained quiet.

"Lacey," I murmured.

"I miss you."

Shit. This was the last thing I needed. I thought we'd moved on from being an item. What should I say? Should I be sympathetic, or take a hard line? Was she getting counseling? Did she need my help?

"Lacey—"

She lifted a cat carrier from under the chair, and I could see Obi's face peering out at me. My chest tightened. Was this some kind of test? A show and tell where she ended up taking Obi away from me. I loved that cat, and she knew that.

"I wanted you to have him; he misses you."

"Lacey?" I couldn't believe what I was hearing, that she was telling me, in a matter-of-fact fashion, that I was able to have Obi back? "For real?" I winced at my own question, aware of the vulnerability in the tone.

"For real, Tate. It's okay, I'm not here to mess with you. I wanted you to have Obi, and to tell you, I'm seeing a counselor." She glanced around her to check the corridor, before moving closer to me. I sensed Vlad move nearer to me. "Can I talk to you privately?"

"You can talk in front of Vlad, he's with me," I thumbed behind me, and she gave me a soft smile.

"With you?"

"We're together."

She smiled then, but the smile was kind of sad. "Good. That's good."

"Are you... is there... "

"Anyone? Not right now. I think I need to focus on me. I don't know what went wrong, but it was a mess from the start."

Guilt consumed me. "I'm sorry I couldn't be what you needed me to be," I offered.

"You're a good man, Tate, but my head... nothing was right. *We* weren't right."

"No, we weren't, but I should have—"

"Stop." She pressed a hand to my chest. "Being seen is what it was all about. The right makeup, the clothes I wore, the way I lived, and the number of followers I had, was everything to me. It was my messed up way of escaping the sadness in my head."

I took her hand and held it. "I'm sorry." I knew all about the pressures of expectation.

"You were my brilliance, Tate." She stopped and bit her lip thoughtfully. "I mean, being with you, it gave me that extra shine. Almost as if I mattered."

"You *do* matter," I said, and grasped her hand. "You mattered to me."

"And you *mattered* to me, but not in a healthy way, and I didn't love you. I wanted to say it face-to-face, I'm sorry." She leaned closer and whispered. "For the lies."

"Get away from him, Lacey!" Marco snapped from the

corridor to the left, coming into the picture and placing himself solidly between me and Lacey, shoving me back. He had a high temper, and a blooming bruise on his left eye, as well as a cut to his lip that needed looking at. "Leave. Her. Alone."

Lacey took his arm. "There wasn't a baby, Marco."

Shit. Why was she bringing that up now? No one had to know that she'd lied, I would never tell a soul if it meant she could have closure in her own mind.

Marco blinked at her and then me. "What? Don't lie for him, Lacey, he's not worth it."

"I'm not. I wanted to keep Tate, and I lied, I think I was looking for... He never hurt me, Marco, but he was there for me when I needed him, and then I hurt him."

Marco raised a hand, I moved, Vlad growled, and Lacey tensed, but Marco wasn't looking at me or Vlad, he was cradling Lacey's face and then pulling her close in a hug.

"Why didn't you come to me? I need you in my life. You're my little sister."

"I couldn't, I didn't want to, I'm so stupid but my head, sometimes nothing makes sense."

Marco held her and closed his eyes, before burying his face in her hair, whispering soft, low words. Vlad and I stood back a little, formed a barrier in case anyone else came out into the hallway, but it was blessedly quiet. When they parted he still held her, and then extended a hand to me, which I shook immediately.

"She says you looked after her," he said.

"I tried."

"I'm sorry."

"It's okay." I said without hesitation.

Marco released his hold of my hand." Vlad?" Behind me Vlad bristled and stepped closer.

"What?"

"You fight like a badass."

I bet he was back there preening like Frank on his perch.

"Of course I do." Vlad stated firmly. "I am Russian animal."

Chapter Fourteen

Vlad

TATE AND I RODE BACK TO THE HOTEL SEPARATELY ON THE bus, his cat in a carrier, purring so loudly I could hear it from where I sat.

It was disappointing but there was no other option. If I sat too close to him I was compelled to touch him in small, territorial ways that still befuddled me. This jealousy and need to stake a claim was as foreign to me as American serving sizes had been when I'd first come to this country. Why must there be four hamburger patties—with bacon— on one bun? And turkey legs that look as if they were removed from an ostrich? *Why?*

I watched Dallas passing by, working my jaw back and forth to ease the ache from a clip from Marco's big fist. That had been a good fight. It had purged some worries from me, clarified things. What it said about me that violence was how I exorcised demons I did not wish to examine too closely. Still, it had served its purpose. The team had been energized and I'd been able to work out some issues. Unable to peek back to see Tate, I nonetheless heard him, his soft Texas twang rising above the masculine chatter. My ears picked it out, much like a mother can differentiate her baby's cry even in a room full of other little ones.

My phone buzzed. I dug into the front pocket of my suit jacket. A text from Tate.

Can we talk? - T

A tiny ball of concern welled up inside my chest. I wrote back that we could talk anytime and told him to come to my room with his virtual playbook. It rankled to have to pretend. He replied with a smiley emoji. I glanced out of the darkened window at the city lights, wishing for something that I suspected I might not have for quite some time. Freedom to be my true self.

The bus rolled up to the hotel, a grand high-rise that seemed to touch the night sky. Truly, everything *was* bigger in Texas. Saying goodnight to the team as we filed into four separate elevators, I shifted my personal bag up on my shoulder higher and commented on some observation Henry was making about chili. Apollo's chili. The boy was so in love. I envied him. Realizing that I grimaced, the taste of my envy bitter on my tongue. Obviously, I had many flaws to work on.

Leaving Henry at the fourth floor, I went to my room, stripped off my suit and tie, and pulled on some rusty-red cotton shorts with the Raptors logo on the left thigh. I eyed the bar but removed a can of lemon-lime soda instead of a tiny bottle of vodka. Then I settled into my chair and waited for the knock. Memories of that first time Tate had come to me rose, sensual recollections that were making me half hard. I shoved at my swelling prick, willing it to go away. Tate wanted to talk, not fuck. I made myself think of my great-grandfather Petro and the time as a child my twin and I had seen him naked. He was an old, old man who hated to wear clothes that pinched his balls or any other part of his body. My father said he was off in the head. He died when we were five, but the memory of his saggy ass was enough to make my dick go soft.

Just in time for the soft knock. I called for him to enter, then realized that I'd not propped the door open as I had previously. I rose and went to open the door. He gave me a wry smile, then entered, his tablet in his hand, the smell of his lemony-orange shampoo and body wash wafting off of him as he passed.

"No sitting in the chair being all dom/sub this time?" he asked when he hit the small lounge area and turned to face me.

"I forget to prop open the door. Were you hoping for that scenario?"

"Maybe."

"Next time, *Zvedva moya.* Where is your cat?"

"Sleeping on my bed. I left a do not disturb sign on the door."

I nodded, then waved at the bed before I dropped my sore, weary ass back into the chair in the corner. Marco had gotten a few good punches in. I felt them in my jaw and lower back. I would wake up with bruises which was business as usual. "Sit. You said you wished to talk?"

He tossed the tablet to the tiny wooden desk, walked to me, fell to his knees, and placed his cheek on my thigh. It was an incredibly touching gesture, one that stirred up hot, slick yearnings. He was learning how to play me. I liked it although I would never confess to that. I ran a finger along his jaw, tracing the bone under the skin.

"Have you come to tell me that you have decided my foolishness no longer appeals?" I gave voice to the screaming fear living deep in my breast.

"No. Of course not." His lashes fluttered as the tips of my fingers moved along the bridge of his nose. "We do need to talk about your jealousy. It's flattering at first but then it becomes..."

He let it dangle. I drew in a long breath through my nose. "Yes, it becomes problematic. I have been thinking about my insecurities when it comes to you." His sleepy eyes flew open. "Don't look so surprised, my star. No other man has captured my heart as you have so I had no cares what they did or with whom. You..." I outlined his sexy lips. His tongue darted out to flick at my finger as it moved across the seam. "You own me even though I am the one who is supposed to be in total control. I see you with younger men, men your own age, men who are able to be out, who could give you the life that you should have, and I fear. I fear that you will grow tired of me, of my inability to be an out gay man. Losing you would kill me."

He pushed up from the floor, his gaze holding mine, and straddled me. I cupped his ass as he sat on my thighs. His hands cradled my face. I stared into his eyes. Such gorgeous eyes. Bright and dark, they enraptured me.

"I'm not going anywhere. I love you. What we have is private. I'm good with that, honestly, no don't scowl." He leaned in to brush his lips over mine. "It's true. I'm all over being in the spotlight. I'm good keeping us to us. I know you being out might bring some hatred down on your family. That would kill me knowing that I'd been a pushy brat and demanded that of you. So, it's just us being private for however long we have to be. If that's when you retire, in like twenty years, then that's cool. I'm not going anywhere."

"If you could feel the aches I'm feeling right now you'd say retirement should happen next week," I joked weakly, giving his high, tight ass a squeeze. "I will work on being less stupid. Give me time to adjust to loving someone."

He swept his lips over mine again, a soft whisper of a kiss that said more delights were to come.

"We'll work it out together. Just the two of us."

"But there are others who know, Tate," I reminded him, kneading the hard buttocks resting in my palms. "Eli, Colorado. Do others suspect?"

His fingers rested on my cheekbones, his thumbs under my chin. "Maybe we need to talk to them. The ones who are going to see us together the most. Just our friends. Ask them to keep it quiet. They'd do that for us. For you especially. They love their captain even when he's being a jealous asshole." I must have frowned. Talking to others about personal things did not feel right to me. "Think on it while you try to be less of an a-hole."

"Ugh, yes, I must work on that as well. One would think when you were in your mid-thirties you would have fewer personal flaws to grow out of, not more. You make me crazy, Tate. What I feel is…I cannot put it into words but it is strong...so strong. It is love so strong. So damn strong."

He kissed me then. It was fire and wet tongues. There was no denying the man when he came to me hard and wanting. I stood, his ass in my hands. With a grunt he grabbed my neck, his lips coming back to mine. The trip to the bed was short but our passion burned for hours.

OCTOBER RACED BY AS DID THE FIRST HALF OF NOVEMBER. Where the time went I wasn't sure. It seemed to be a whirlwind of travel, hockey, and a massive pre-Halloween party at Colorado's sprawling mansion. He and the younger players performed, in costume and on film, two songs from a movie that I'd only just seen two days prior, the *Rocky Horror Picture Show*. I had a small part as a man in suit with a pointer and a paper on a board with dance steps. My lines were about stepping left and right and making your knees come in tight. I felt moronic but then I saw Colorado in a corset and fishnet stockings belting out a song about being from Transylvania. I felt less silly after seeing that performance. The man had great legs for stockings and high heels. The team released the video on Halloween and it trended within an hour. All of our social media pages gained new viewers, or so Sebastian kept telling us via text. I did little on social media, preferring to keep my life private for obvious reasons.

Not only were our social media pages scoring, we were doing so on the ice as well. Over the past month we'd slowly and methodically clawed our way to being well within a wildcard slot, if the playoffs were held now, which they were not. April was a long way off but we'd started clicking as a team. Perhaps I was biased but I credited much of it to Tate. He'd been that missing link, that final puzzle piece that we'd been searching for. With two big top lines and respectable third and fourth lines, we were chalking up the offensive stats. The defense was also doing well. Eli and I had second place in the standings for blocked shots, an honor that was obvious whenever we stripped off our clothes. We also were racking up high hits and a low PIM/G—penalty minutes per game—rating. Spending less time in the penalty box made Coach happy. I'd manage to sock in two goals in six weeks, bringing my grand total of goals to three for the season so far. As much as I would have loved to be one of those flashy offensive defensemen like they had in Harrisburg, Pittsburgh, and Washington, my cloth was a different fiber and I was happy being that big Russian everyone tried to avoid but few could. Although I would confess to enjoying the rush of scoring when it happened.

With Thanksgiving looming on the horizon, Tate and I decided to have a small gathering with the men who we were closest to on the team. We'd been able to keep things between us hidden but wished to let our friends know, swearing them to secrecy. It was much easier to light a small containment fire which we could control than to have someone say something offhandedly and ignite a roaring wildfire. With that philosophy in mind, we all decided to spend our last free day before the big American holiday together. Tate had arranged for one of his neighbors to tend to Obi as we'd be gone all day, the same person who checked in when the team was on the road.

Thankfully, we were not slated to play on Thanksgiving. That honor went to the Railers who would be in New York City playing what was touted as a "showdown game". Big city, big teams, big ratings. The Raptors were none of those things. Yet.

With two Jeeps packed with food, beer, and rowdy hockey players, we roared out of Tucson early in the morning and headed to the Saguaro National Park. I had been to the national park a few times since coming to Arizona, but it was the first time for Tate. Rock music blared out of the speakers in Colorado's blue Jeep. Alex had his own Jeep and was toting Ryker, Jacob, Eli, and Sebastian. Tate and I were riding in the back with a chattering Apollo Vasquez between us. Henry was riding shotgun, as the Americans called it, and Penn was driving. He drove much like he played hockey. Erratically but laced with greatness. It was a busy day at the park, due to the holiday, but we kept off the main trails.

Tate marveled at the sights. The massive mountains, the towering Saguaro cactus, the birds and snakes and wildlife we spotted as we bounced along. His brown eyes were alive, his smile wide. I longed to kiss him simply for the joy seeing him so happy brought to me. But...

"Okay so pick the site and we'll start roasting some wieners," Penn shouted as he looked back to grin at us. The Jeep nearly ran off the road before he righted it. Apollo was halfway in my lap, his eyes wide as hubcaps. If not for the seatbelt he would have been wrapped around my neck like a scarf. "Roads. Who needs them? I say a man should make his own way in life! Do what he wants, when he wants, where he wants."

With that we went off-road for a few miles until we skidded up to a campsite that was far away from the beaten path. A lone grill stood next to a weathered log cabin camp. Since we'd not gotten a camping permit, we'd not go into the cabin.

"Fuck yeah!" Colorado hooted, leaping out of the Jeep as I worked to peel Apollo from me. He was quite strong for such a small man. Finally, I got him loose and pointed in the direction of Henry who was paler than I had ever seen him. I leaned out of the Jeep and slapped Penn across the back of his head. He yelped. "Dude, seriously nasty way to harsh the buzz."

"Some of us do not appreciate bad rides," I snarled, jerking my head at Henry who was holding Apollo close to him as one would a buoy in a turbulent sea.

"Oh. Shit. Sorry man. Cy, you should have said something. Okay, no more off road for us! Grab the charcoal. I'll get the tunes and the beer!"

With that pronouncement our goalie raced off after lifting a cooler and his battered acoustic guitar out of the back.

"I swear that man cares about no one other than himself," I muttered to Tate who could do nothing but nod.

We unpacked the Jeeps and began our manly day out with a game of touch Frisbee. Touch meaning tackle. The temperature was a dry seventy-two degrees, perfect weather to be outside. After the game, which my team won, we went for a long hike, Alex reading off facts about the park, flora and fauna from his phone as we walked. We saw cactus as tall as a giraffe, small birds, a king snake warming himself on a rock, and several pronghorn off in the distance. When we returned to our makeshift camp we were all starving. Thank the stars that Apollo had packed more than just hot dogs and mustard. There were dishes of spicy Mexican food that we dove into, followed by a tres leches cake that was so delicious I had three helpings.

The memory of a small pool of crystal clear water nearby called to us, and so we all walked to it, hoping to work off some of the food we'd gorged on. The water had been warmed by the sun but was refreshing on bare feet and calves. Soon the boys fell into splashing and trying to dunk each other even though the pool was barely two feet deep. I was pulled in and then had to fight my way back to the rock where I'd been digesting my feast. Tate leaped onto my back, Ryker latched onto a leg, and Jacob plus Eli tackled me around the waist. It was the heft of the big farm boy and my defensive partner that knocked me off my feet. I came sputtering up, my clothes soaked, my lover scrambling to his bare feet. A small skirmish broke out during which I showed them all that the old dog still had what it took to handle the young pups.

Colorado arrived at dusk, guitar in hand, and flopped down on the rocks we'd been stretched out on as we dried off. The rock star gave us all a smiling assessment.

"You guys are like the rock center of my world." He rapped knuckles with Ryker who was resting his head on Jacob's belly. I found myself staring at Tate, who was leaning back on his arms, face to the softly darkening sky, hair knotted from water play. I'd never seen him so beautiful aside from when I was making love to him. It was now or never, I decided.

"Tate and I are lovers," I blurted out.

All eyes swiveled from Colorado who'd been tuning his guitar to us.

"Old news," Eli said around a fake yawn.

I gave him a look that made him snigger.

"And?" Ryker asked, his cheek pillowed on his fiancé's stomach.

"And we would like you all to know because we feel you are all our rock centers as well."

There. I'd done it. I'd come out. Sort of. In a microscopic way. Tate sat up straight, his eyes moving around the small circle of our teammates and friends.

"We really need you guys to keep it to yourselves though, okay? Vlad has some touchy issues with his family and his homeland and I'm totally tapped out with drama," Tate said, his sight lingering on Apollo who was fussing with some chipped polish on his toe. Henry nudged him.

Apollo's deep brown eyes flew from his pedicure to the group. "Oh, yes, sorry. My toes are frightful. School is killing my downtime. Yes, of course. Do you think we would *ever* out someone who wasn't ready to be out?" Apollo asked. We all shook our heads.

"Thank you," Tate replied for both of us.

"Dude, we all totally get it. I mean I know what kind of hell Stan went through. We got your backs," Ryker said, petting Jacob's belly as one would a pillow, then nestling back in. The small group all murmured along in agreement.

"I'm deeply touched that you two felt safe enough with

us to tell us what we all already knew," Colorado said as he began strumming, then launched into a song about friendships, rock centers, and cool desert nights. Then in front of them all I wiggled closer to Tate and put my arm around his shoulder. He let his head drop to mine. It was everything that I had ever dreamed it could be but a thousand times better.

Chapter Fifteen

Tate

WHO KNEW I HAD AN ACCENT?

"You sound like a Ewing," Alex said.

"What is a *Ewing*?" Vlad asked, and after that a games night at my place had deteriorated in a heated debate about eighties TV Shows, none of which we'd been alive for. Well, apart from Vlad who'd been born in eighty-six but I'm not sure how much of the US eighties had hit rural Russia, or even the nineties.

"And then he was in the shower," Eli read out from Wikipedia, poking at his screen and snorting a laugh, "And it was all a dream."

"A whole season?"

"Who the fuck knows."

"That man was all hat and no cattle," Colorado did a perfect Texan drawl. "Bit like our Tate hereabouts when ya'lls madder than a wet hen."

I think he was messing up his abouts and his y'alls, but

he'd spent ten minutes working on his ya'lls from his y'alls and that had stopped the game of poker and deteriorated into me not being able to breathe through laughter. He was a funny dude, and somehow he had us all singing Dolly Parton songs until midnight in which we all had to pretend to be from Texas. Again, messing up the accents, and mixing Tennessee with Texas, but who the hell cared at this point? We just let Colorado do his thing and enjoyed the laughter it caused.

My home was in Minnesota, and tonight was the first night of bye week, an entire five days off where Vlad and I planned on going back to stay at my parents' place, meet up with Logan and Josie, and various nieces and nephews, and the dogs, and even though Vlad loved me, I wasn't sure how long that was going to last after he got a good look at the rest of the Collins clan. Apollo and Henry were cat-sitting Obi, Frank was being cared for by Tom and Mona, our bags were packed, and we were flying to Minnesota early tomorrow. In fact, I wasn't sure we'd even go to bed tonight.

When everyone left, we cleared up a little, but not long enough to dissuade me from being tugged to the bedroom. So, it was a yes on the bed, then.

"Your accent turns my insides out," Vlad stuttered when we lay on our backs staring at the ceiling, hot and sticky and coming down from a high.

I curled up on my side, and kissed him soundly. "So does yours."

I was right about not sleeping; there was no point, since we needed to be at Tucson International by five a.m., and it was already three. Grabbing our bags and locking up the house, we headed for the airport, chatting quietly in the new dawn, and taking our seats up front in first class. The flight was just over seven hours and Vlad was a big man, so this was my treat.

After all, he was running the gauntlet of my family.

"Big brother, Logan, wife, Gemma, two daughters, Lizzie and Bella. Middle sister, Josie, partner, David, not married, but engaged, son Mitchell. Dogs, and various cats, your mom is named Elizabeth, your dad is Francis. Not shortened to Frank like my Frank."

"You can stop saying all that now," I was amused at the way he was attempting to remember everything before he'd even met my family.

He turned to look at me his pale eyes focused. "I will not mess this up."

I elbowed him, difficult with the distance between these seats, and he raised an eyebrow. "Big brother, Logan…"

I tuned him out, disrupted by yet more food being offered, and a helpful attendant who was a hockey fan and wanted to know about the Raptors' chance of getting to the cup run.

"We will get to the playoffs." Vlad was defiant, and at least it got him off the subject of my family and remembering their names.

"I'm a Railers fan," she began.

"Someone has to be," Vlad muttered under his breath, and I kicked him as subtly as I could.

"I love Tennant Rowe, and Stan, he's the best goalie. I think we have a good chance of the cup this year—"

"Uhmm, could I get some more chips?" I interrupted,

as kindly as I could without breaking every polite bone in my body.

Vlad muttered something in Russian, but at least the attendant left to get me what I'd asked, and by the time she returned, I'd gotten Vlad back to repeating family names, added to which we only had another ten minutes until we landed. The Raptors had been having a good run of games, much to everyone's surprise, winning five out of the last twelve games outright, and getting points in two others for taking the game to overtime.

I knew the media were saying that I was the savior of the team, that it was me arriving which had changed things. After games, it was me who was being asked all the questions.

But they were wrong; it wasn't just me.

Under Vlad, and with Coach, and the management behind us, this team was a unit. We worked hard, we laughed, we commiserated, we learned from our mistakes; it reminded me of all the positive team rebuilds of the past. Okay, so maybe this year we wouldn't make it all the way to the cup, but we wouldn't be bottom, and that was because we were a damn good team.

As soon as the seatbelt light went out I was up from my seat and grabbing coats from the overhead bin. Minnesota was cold compared to Arizona, but when I passed the coat to Vlad he muttered again. He'd been doing that a lot, telling me that there was no way Minnesota was as cold as where he'd come from, and he'd been there before. Then he half smiled at me and shrugged on the coat, doing it for me.

God I wanted to kiss him.

"Good luck in the run to the cup," our attendant said.

"Yes, good luck to your Railers," Vlad said very politely, and then I hoped to hell the poor woman didn't speak Russian because whatever came next sounded a lot like what came out of the beak of an angry parrot called Frank.

We made it to arrivals after a short wait, and there they were, the entire Collins clan, holding up a huge sign, *Welcome Home Tot.*

I will literally kill *my brother.*

The hugs were wonderful, and at first I encouraged Vlad right in there, but he was like this huge blond teddy bear, swinging up children, hugging my sister, doing this awesome bow and hand kiss thing to Mom, shaking hands in all seriousness with Dad. By the time we reached the convoy of cars in the parking lot, Vlad might as well have changed his last name to Collins.

We were in Logan's SUV, me wedged between Lizzie and Bella, and Vlad taking shotgun. It wasn't as if his huge ass would fit in between my wriggly nieces, and this way I got to hear all about princesses and parties and how brilliant it was that I was here for Lizzie's birthday and was I okay to dress up as a prince. Given that I would do anything for my nieces and nephews, I immediately said yes.

Then I heard Vlad and Logan talking, and I zoned out on princess parties and focused right in on Vlad's questions about me.

"...so that is why he has a scar on his knee." I heard Logan finish, and groaned. I so didn't want Vlad to hear about the time I was on roller skates and ended up on my ass in a bramble bush in our old house. In my defense I'd been two at the time, and Logan had shoved me, but I bet he'd never added that part.

"I have another question," Vlad said.

Logan laughed loudly, "Is it about why he can't watch horror movies and the whole *Woman in Black* thing?"

"Stop it Logan, that movie was scary sh—" I stopped myself swearing, but Lizzie glanced up at me with her nearly six-year-old wisdom and raised an eyebrow. Damn this family!

"No," Vlad said, "But we can come back to that. I wanted to know why do you call Tate this name, Tot."

I saw my brother side-eye Vlad. *Fuck my life.*

Logan snorted a laugh. "Because he's a Tate-r Tot."

"Tater Tot," Vlad said, all serious, but I caught his gaze in the mirror and he was smiling. "Like those squishy potato things?"

"Best food EVER!" Lizzie shouted.

I groaned dramatically, and closed my eyes. I swore after this break, Vlad would never be able to look at me the same way again.

"Did Tate ever tell you about getting drunk and wanting to adopt all the legless kittens of the world?"

"No, please tell me more."

It was like that all the way back to Mom and Dad's place, and by the time we arrived I didn't think there was a single embarrassing story left to share.

Dinner was loud, chaotic, a mess of love and hugs, and news about schools and work. Vlad and I didn't come out and officially say we were a couple, but the adults knew, and it wasn't safe to have PDAs in case one of the kids went to school and said something. I knew we were being paranoid, but that was what secrets did to a person. At least we sat next to each other and our knees bumped as we ate.

Logan tapped a fork on his glass and one by one every person fell silent.

"I wanted to raise a toast," he began, and I helped Mitchell fill his sippy cup with some of the special juice that my sister had placed next to him. I didn't know what we were toasting, but all of the family should be involved. Even Vlad picked up his water glass. "To Tate," he began, and everyone stared at me as I blinked back at them in surprise. Then my brother, god damn his heart, looked right at Vlad. "And to Vlad."

"We're so happy for Vlad and you..." Mom began.

"... that the Raptors are doing so well," Dad finished, as if they'd rehearsed it.

They were toasting us as a couple, making it so it wasn't obvious, and I wanted to thank them but all I could do was raise my glass in salute, the same as Vlad.

"We will get a wildcard place," Vlad announced.

I didn't disbelieve him, and by the nods around the table everyone else was utterly convinced.

"There's something else," Josie said, before the table was reduced back to its chaotic state. She put her hand under the table and David, her partner, put his arm around her shoulder. She held up her hand to show the shiny ring, and then held up a hand when we all began to congratulate them. "And we're expecting." More congratulations, and then everyone went quiet when she suddenly burst into tears. "It's twins, and I'm so happy."

Mom bustled around to hug her, and the two of them hugged it out.

"She is happy," David confirmed, "but she's like super emotional. Last night she ate an entire tub of—"

"Don't tell them that!" Josie cried, and then began to laugh. When she and David hugged it was pure beauty and my heart ached with it.

I was going to be an uncle again. I touched Vlad's thigh hoping he would take my hand and hold it. He laced his fingers in mine.

"I love my family," I admitted, and when I looked into his gorgeous eyes, he smiled.

"I love your family, too."

We were staying at my parents' house, in two separate rooms, but that wouldn't last long, and Mom and Dad knew. Not that we could do anything but hug because the thought of doing anything more freaked me out, but at least we were together.

He proved it when he wore pointy ears at the princess party and pretended he was a giant. He also never said a single word when Lizzie demanded he allow ten six-year-olds to paint his face. They made him an ogre, with green skin, and his white-blond hair was flecked with red. They made sure his horns weren't going to fall off, and he sat there and he stared at me and I was more in love with him with each second he didn't move.

The ogre was the hit of the party, particularly when he was vanquished and I couldn't see him under a heap of Disney princesses. Which is when they turned on me and declared I was going to be a prince for real.

When we snuggled into bed that night, we ended up

finding just how much glitter there was on us both, despite showers, and how the green might not come off the bit behind his ear. I didn't want to mention that I thought one of the girls might have been using a permanent marker.

He patted the area. "It's okay," he rumbled, trying to whisper. "We will get to the playoffs, and my beard will hide it."

Playoffs were weeks away yet, we wouldn't know if we'd gotten a place until April, and it would rest on so many factors as to whether we made it in as one of the 'best of the rest' wildcard places.

Stranger things had happened in hockey history.

We still had flecks of glitter when we wrapped up for pond hockey. On my parents' land, not much more than an acre, but resting in front of the trees there was a large pond which was frozen solid, and already carried the marks of blades. Lizzie was a demon on her skates, and I exchanged glances with her dad as Logan rolled his eyes. Logan used to play shinny hockey in the winter just to stay in shape for baseball and Josie skated a little here and there when she wasn't in an acting class or on a stage somewhere, Lizzie had the Collins genes, and we went toe to toe on a couple of occasions; she was a canny operator, using a combination of big woobly eyes, and her height to get past Vlad twice.

"You can't fall for the eyes, dude," Logan warned him after the second time.

Lizzie shoved her dad from behind and all three of them ended up bundling into a snowbank, Vlad on the bottom.

All I can say is that I was sure it washed off most of the remaining glitter.

We separated into two teams for a snowball fight, Vlad and I on opposing sides. Getting a face full of snow was worth it if the two of us were rolling in the white stuff. Losing to Vlad's team was a bit of a shit, but my big sister was missing from my team, and Josie had a demon throwing arm.

By the time we went back to the house for everything that was laid out–cookies, hot chocolate, cakes of all kinds, sandwiches, and chips–Josie had her feet up and was eating from a tub of Ben and Jerry's, I reached for Vlad's hand and squeezed it. So brief a person could've missed it. But the touch was enough.

ON THE FLIGHT BACK TO ARIZONA WE WERE BOTH QUIET and lost in thought, and thankfully none of the attendants were hockey fans, not in the slightest.

"Someday I would like a family," Vlad murmured, and I turned to face him.

"For real?"

"I'm thirty-five, I'm ready to…" He frowned. "How many more years do I have? In hockey, I mean?"

My chest constricted, imagining a team without Vlad.

"We need to get the cup first," I encouraged.

"Maybe we will, maybe we won't, but one day I'd like to work with teenagers, not babies, not little ones, but the ones who are questioning, or scared, who want to play hockey, or ballet, who need someone. That would be my family."

I nodded. "That would be a wonderful family."

"And you'd be there as well."

We didn't have to touch to look each other in the eyes, our gazes locked.

"I'll be right by your side."

Epilogue

Vlad

THERE WASN'T MUCH THAT COULD LURE ME FROM A WARM bed with an ever warmer Tate sharing it with me. Aside from Easter service. Even knowing I wished to rise and attend mass, I lingered there for a few moments, enjoying the way the sun was warming his face, highlighting the small glints of russet in his dark hair, and shining on the fading love bite that I'd left on his right buttock a few nights ago. Unable to stop myself, I cupped that firm cheek and my dick began to fatten up. Knowing if I lingered much longer Tate's body would keep me abed, I pulled away from temptation. When I spoke to my mother later today she would ask if I'd been to church and I would have to say I had not. Then I would be scolded. So, yes, leaving bed and Tate simply had to take place.

In Russia, our *Pashka*, or Easter, is one of the biggest holy days. Even bigger than Christmas. The faithful and the atheists, the young and old, the rich and poor, all attend

Easter Mass. And so it was that I'd woken up groggy after a late night celebrating our wild card slot with our teammates to attend church even though I longed for more sleep. We had worked hard to get here, but the fates had also been kind. Our team had turned things around after the All-Star break in late January. We'd burrowed in deep and fought tooth and nail for every damn win we could get our greedy hands on. Climbing slowly out of the muck at the bottom of our division point by point. Last night's celebration at Colorado's had been well warranted. Even Coach had shown up with Mark, to kick up their heels. He wore a white cowboy hat which held some sort of American symbolism to him, although he was Canadian. No one ever said hockey players made sense.

Securing that wildcard position in the Pacific division had been a convoluted affair which had come down to us having to win and two other teams having to lose, as well as mathematical equations and three spits over my left shoulder for luck. We would be facing off against a physical Las Vegas Rollers team in two days. Our flight to Vegas left early tomorrow so Tate and I could share a holiday dinner at my condo, just him, me, Frank, and Obi. I was looking forward to this brief respite from the rigors of hockey, and some time in a house of worship. It had been a year. It was time.

I'd not been able to locate a Russian Orthodox church, but had found a small Greek Orthodox church in the Catalina Foothills. While I didn't go often I did make a point to go at Easter, even though my American friends had already celebrated it a week earlier. Different calendars made for a confusing time of things. I felt a yearly meeting with God in his house was reasonable. I had much to thank the Maker for this year. I showered, shaved, dressed nicely, and left a note for Tate on my pillow.

As I cruised to church, Taylor was singing "Gorgeous" and I had to smile at the lyrics and how they made me think of my lover. Yes, Tate was gorgeous, and open, and submissive, and mine. Fully and without question, even if we had separate addresses and were unable to display our affection for each other in public.

We'd become quite good at subterfuge over the past several months. Telling my neighbors that he often had to spend a few days with me because of his place being fumigated for bugs, or being painted, or having to have plumbing work done. They had to wonder why he lived in such a terribly unkempt home. In truth, Tate was at my place more than his own anymore, which was why Obi now travelled with him. And why my parrot now hissed like a cat, then cackled like a maniac. The cat and the macaw were having some issues but with slow progress they were working out the kinks. Much like their owners. Most days we were fine with our lives and the secret we shared with only a select few but some days—birthdays or anniversaries or Valentine's—were difficult. But we do not always get to have everything we desire in life. We would make do until I retired. Then we would see what the world condition was like and if my country had shifted from hatred to more acceptance. If not, then we would move onward somehow.

The church appeared on my left, a tiny thing with a lovely steeple. Its white clapboards stood out against the desert pinks, purples, and tans that the noonday sun was bringing to life. I parked, dropped my keys into my front pocket, and weaved my way through the mass of cars in the packed parking lot. I slipped into the cool, dark interior, blessed myself right to left as I'd been taught, and then found a spot to sit in as the priest led the congregation in an opening prayer. Throughout the mass I kept to myself, head bowed, mind on my conversation with the Lord. While a few people may have thought they recognized me, for the most part I had time to reflect, thank God for the blessings he had given me, and ask him to possibly look over the Raptors, as we were good men who had worked *so* hard to right our sinking ship. God did love a reformed sinner, and no team in the league had sinned so badly or had worked so much for redemption as we had.

When the mass was over I left as silently as I had entered, fished out my phone, and turned it back on. A flood of texts came in from the team, my brother, and Tate thanking me for the ass rub before I left but wondering why just the one cheek and not his cock. Blushing as I read his dirty text a mere ten meters from church, I smiled, nonetheless. Such a tease he was. I loved it, just as I loved him.

I hurried home, eager to eat as I'd only had a slice of toast and a cup of coffee before leaving so we could have a traditional Russian Easter meal when I returned. I'd ordered in all manner of delicious foods from a Russian restaurant in Phoenix. It included *Pashka,* which was a dish made of curd cheese, nuts, raisins, and candied fruit shaped into a truncated pyramid to symbolize the tomb of

Christ. We also had *Kulich*, a leavened consecrated Easter bread, beautifully decorated hardboiled eggs, and of course *Makovnik*, which was a poppy seed cake. Later we would feast on spring leg of lamb stuffed with garlic and anchovies, potato galette, and horseradish carrot salad. It had all looked wonderful when it had arrived. Tate had given the food a worrisome glance while muttering about a plain old honey ham with scalloped potatoes. *Americans.* So rigid about their oversized foods. He would have to learn to try Russian dishes if my plans for the summer came to fruition. As I pulled into my driveway, I pondered if I should tell him what my twin and I had discussed a week ago or keep it as a surprise. Perhaps an Easter gift would be nice...

As soon as I stepped into my house, I found my arms filled with Tate Collins. It was an enthusiastic greeting, his mouth finding mine as Frank chased the cat through the condo.

"Mm, this is nice," I whispered over his kiss-slick lips. "I was only gone for two hours."

"Two long hours with a cat and a macaw squabbling. It's like having two kids."

He took me by the hand and led me to the sofa. "One cannot stuff a kid into a cage and give him a seed stick to chew on when he is being bad, at least to my knowledge."

He sat and tugged me down beside him. I flopped to the couch with a grunt, wiggling to face him. His hair was damp, his cheeks unshaven, his cocoa eyes infused with warmth as he gazed at me.

"True. When we have our kids we'll get them a playpen."

"Is that not much the same thing?" I teased, reaching up to touch his beautiful face. "I love that we talk now of children. How we will accomplish it I cannot say, but hearing you speak of that future with me fills my heart. I feel as if the heavens come to life in my breast when you say such things."

He scrambled over me, pushing me back into the cushions to kiss me until my breath was coming in huffs.

"Are we still doing the *Star Wars* film marathon today, or do you want to do other things?" His question was a silly one. My stiff prick was already saying what it wished to do with this one day off.

"Hmm, a movie about robots that be-boop-boop and laser swords—"

"Light sabers."

"Ah, yes, light sabers. A movie about robots that be-boop-boop and *light sabers* or taking you back to my bed and tying you to the headboard. My, that *is* a most difficult decision."

His gaze ignited. "Is that what those silk scarves you bought are for?"

"Perhaps. If you're good and do as you're told."

"Don't I always?" He slithered off me, then made his way to the bedroom, tossing back hot looks as I slowly got to my feet. I'd tell him about the trip to Russia in the summer to meet my family later. Right now I was craving sugar.

THE END

Next for the Raptors

School and Rock (Raptors 5)

When Colorado Penn finds an unexpected package on his front step, his life will be changed forever.

Colorado Penn is living the dream. Starting goalie for the Arizona Raptors when in season, lead singer for a hard rock band when summer rolls around. He's the quintessential free spirit who's making sure to enjoy all the carnal blessings of his athleticism and gritty singing voice. Now the Raptors are moving into their first playoff appearance in years, but the arrival of an unexpected package means that hockey may have to take a backseat to something way more important. Instead of the usual undergarments from adoring fans, he finds a newborn baby with a small note tucked under her carrier, naming him as the father. He refuses to give up his daughter and is determined to be the kind of father he'd dreamed of having. But to keep Madeline, he'll need help, and he'll need it fast. Enter handsome emergency manny, Joseph.

They may be opposites, but Colorado starts to see that Joseph's stable, calm influence makes his chaotic lifestyle choices seem less appealing. There's something about the man that soothes not only his infant daughter but also the wild child inside Colorado.

Joseph is one year away from getting his degree in planetary science, working cover shifts at the planetarium, and pulling in income with short term manny gigs. Stars collide as he provides emergency childcare for the wild man of hockey, a man who moves so fast through life that he doesn't know how to stop. Homeless, and caring for his niece, Emma, fate brings Joseph into Colorado and baby Madeline's life. Madeline is a sweetheart, and Colorado is trying his hardest to make the best decision for his baby girl. He offers his home to Joseph and Emma and an indecent salary, to keep them in his life until summer's end. Colorado brings mysticism and metal to Joseph's sanctuary of science, but somehow Joseph needs to tame this shooting star and create a family. Nothing in the contract said Joseph had to fall in love to make that happen, but when it's time for him and his niece to leave, will the void in his heart ever heal, or will it remain as cold as space itself?

Hockey Series' from RJ Scott & V.L. Locey

Harrisburg Railers

Owatonna U Hockey

Arizona Raptors

Boston Rebels

LA Storm

Chesterford Coyotes - Young Adult

Harrisburg Railers

When hockey wunderkind Tennant Rowe meets his new coach, he knows he's in trouble. Jared Madsen is nine years older than Tennant, impossibly attractive, and — worst of all — his brother's off-limits best friend. Is their chemistry worth the risk?

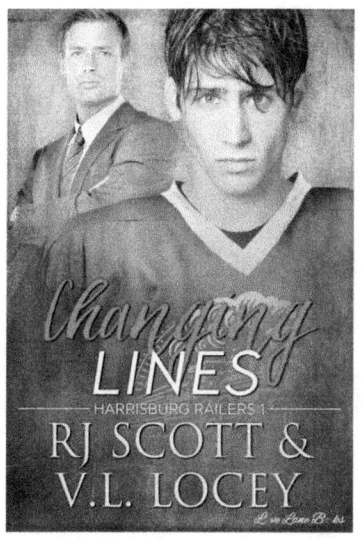

Changing Lines (Railers 1)

Can Tennant show Jared that age is just a number, and that love is all that matters?

The Rowe Brothers are famous hockey hotshots, but as the youngest of the trio, Tennant has always had to play against his brothers' reputations. To get out of their shadows, and against their advice, he accepts a trade to the Harrisburg Railers, where he runs into Jared Madsen. Mads is an old family friend and his brother's one-time teammate. Mads is Tennant's new coach. And Mads is the sexiest thing he's ever laid eyes on.

Jared Madsen's hockey career was cut short by a fault in his heart, but coaching keeps him close to the game. When Ten is traded to the team, his carefully organized world is thrown into chaos. Nine years his junior and his best friend's brother, he knows Ten is strictly off-limits, but as soon as he sees Ten's moves, on and off the ice, he knows that his heart could get him into trouble again.

Changing Lines

Harrisburg Railers (Hockey Romance)

1. Changing Lines
2. First Season
3. Deep Edge
4. Poke Check
5. Last Defense
6. Goal Line
7. Neutral Zone
8. Hat Trick
9. Save The Date
10. Baby Makes Three
11. Rivals
12. Perfect Gifts

13. Family First

Railers Volume 1 | Railers Volume 2 | Railers Volume 3 | Railers Volume 4

Meet the men of Owatonna University's hockey team

Ryker (Owatonna U, 1)

Ryker

Ryker is hockey royalty, Jacob is a poor country boy. Can two vastly different people find common ground and become the men they want to be?

Ryker comes from a long line of championship-winning hockey players. Playing college hockey to develop his game is his only focus, and nothing will stand in the way of him working to become the best player. He has no room for relationships, people who point out his flaws, or anyone who calls him on his dreams. He certainly has no place for love, and meeting Jacob is nothing but a useful distraction on the side. After all trying to get his Owatonna Eagles teammate into bed is less work and more play. When tragedy rocks his family, his charmed life crumbles, and the only person he can turn to is the same one who claims to hate him.

Jacob Benson has only known hard work and stifling conservative values his whole life. Born and raised in the small rural community of Eden Crossing, Minnesota, he's the only son of a hard-working but struggling dairy farming family. Jacob is using his skills in hockey to finance his way to an agricultural science degree. These four years at Owatonna U. will probably be the only time he has to enjoy life, gain acceptance about his sexuality, and live openly before his inevitable return to the farm. Running into a pretty rich boy like Ryker Madsen is putting a damper on his enjoyment of life away from home. Ryker's flip, conceited, carefree attitude grates on Jacob's every nerve. So why, if Ryker is everything he dislikes, does he want nothing more than to explore the sinful dreams that his annoying teammate stars in every night?

Ryker

Owatonna U Hockey (Hockey Romance)

1. Ryker
2. Scott

Coast to Coast (Arizona Raptors 1)

Coast To Coast

When opposites attract, this bottom-of-the-league team will never be the same again.

A stipulation in his father's will forces Mark back into the arms of a family that disowned him and leaves him one-third owner of a hockey team facing financial ruin. He doesn't even watch hockey, let alone like it, and wants nothing more than to head back to New York. Then there's the new coach, a stubborn, opinionated, irritating man with superiority issues and questionable music taste. Butting heads with Rowen becomes the new normal, but it comes with passionate debate and an all-consuming lust.

Challenged to rebuild one of the worst teams in the league into a future cup contender, Rowen can't pass up the opportunity. Never in his twenty years of hockey has he ever seen a team managed so badly or coached players overflowing with resentment and bigotry. Yet there's something about this team and this city that compels him to roll up his sleeves and start dismantling. If only Mark, one of three siblings who now own the Raptors, wasn't so damned rock-headed yet so damned appealing his job might be easier. It doesn't look like either is willing to give in, but one night in a dark, desert hotel changes everything.

Coast To Coast

Arizona Raptors (Hockey Romance)

1. Coast To Coast
2. Across the Pond
3. Shadow and Light
4. Sugar and Ice
5. School and Rock

Top Shelf (Boston Rebels 1)

Top Shelf

Acting on the attraction to his best friend's brother has always been off the table for Xander until a passionate hookup with Mason at a beach resort begins a love affair that burns long after summer ends.

Mason specializes in assisting same-sex couples on their journey to becoming parents and fighting every rule that blocks his way in the stuck-in-the-past agency that hired him. Living in his brother's pool house is rent-free, and every cent he earns he saves for his dream—that one day he'd have his own company helping others. The downside is that he has to see his annoying brother every day, the upside is that his brother's teammates from the Boston Rebels make regular visits. The eye candy that passes Mason's window is almost enough to make him consider dating a hockey player, but not just any player though. Ever since Xander —his brother's childhood friend—came out as gay at a press conference, Mason's puppy love has turned into a burning attraction he can no longer ignore.

Hockey has been one of Xander's main focuses since he was old enough to balance on skates. Well, hockey and Mason Kingsley, but Mason was always unattainable. Now that he's about to see thirty candles on his birthday cake and is no longer hiding the fact he's gay, he's ready to find a soul mate to make his life complete. A summer vacation is just what he needs to have time to think, but when the Boston Rebels arriving in paradise with Mason in tow, thinking is the last thing he needs. One torrid night under a balmy moon and rules about not messing with his best friend's brother vanish on a warm, tropical breeze.

Summer romances don't generally last past Labor Day, but with the new season about to begin Xander and Mason are going to have to face the world and decide if their love is real enough to withstand everything.

Top Shelf

Boston Rebels

Lost In Boston (Free Prequel Novella)

1. Top Shelf
2. Back Check
3. Snowed
4. Royal Lines
5. Blade
6. Rental

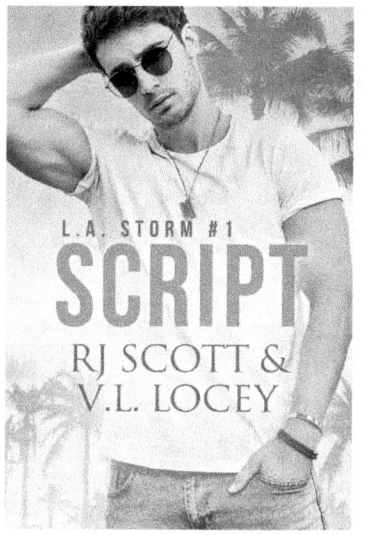

Script (LA Storm, 1)

Script

**Hollywood A-lister Finn might be Canadian, but he needs
Cameron to show him how to hockey.**

Actor Finn Kerrigan is at a crossroads. After growing up a soap
star, then starring in a hugely successful trilogy of action movies,
he's finally given the chance to read a heartfelt and passionate
script that could change his life forever. The role would be
enough for people to see him as a serious actor, and maybe even
win him an award or two (and no, a golden raspberry award for

his action movies doesn't count). Once established as a serious actor he's sure he can come out of the closet and finally live his truth. When he lies to get the part of a hockey player on a struggling team, he suddenly has nowhere to hide. He might be Canadian, but the last time he skated he was ten, and no, he doesn't have hockey in his blood. With only a month until filming starts, he about to be exposed, but partnered with a player who's supposed to be giving him tips, he doesn't realize how many of his secrets will come to light. Falling in lust, one heated kiss at a time, is inevitable, but giving Cameron up at the end of the shoot could break his heart.

Cameron Chavkin is the face of the LA Storm. And the body, and the hair, and the smile. He's at the prime of his career, men and women want to be with him, and he's skating better than he ever has before. His house sits next to a famous rock star's mansion, his garage is filled with expensive cars, and he's even been asked to mentor a once-famous actor in a new hockey movie. Life is pretty sweet. Until the bad boy of hockey meets Finn, a man on the edge with more secrets than Cameron has endorsements. Knowing better than to get involved, Cameron is swept up despite himself, and when it's time to say goodbye to the Storm's most eligible bachelor is finding it hard to follow the script.

Script

LA Storm

1. Script
2. Second
3. *Shield*

4. *Spiral*

Off The Ice (Chesterford Coyotes, 1)

Off The Ice

**A coming-of-age love story with high school, hockey rivalry,
friendship, family, and coming out.**

Soren's life changes in an instant when he and his younger
brother are adopted by hockey royalty. Making sense of his new
life is hard enough, but when he's enrolled in a private school it
means facing a whole new set of problems. Navigating
friendship, family, and hockey is one thing, but being attracted to
the boy who vexes him is a whole new thing.

Felix has a reputation to protect. He's the kid who seems to have everything but looks can be deceiving. Spinning lies about his perfect life, he's created a fantasy world that even he has started to believe. Only, it's not long before everything crumbles, all of his pretty lies are revealed, and only his closest rival sees through his pain and stands by him.

Fighting is easy, friendship is hard, but love is everything.

Off The Ice

Chesterford Coyotes

1. Off The Ice
2. On Thin Ice
3. *Dance on Ice*

Also By RJ Scott

For a full list of ebooks and links please scan the code above or visit rjscott.co.uk/rjbooks

Meet RJ Scott

RJ discovered romance in books at a very young age and realized that if there wasn't romance on the page, she could create it in her head. With over one hundred and fifty books published, she is a full time author of gay romance.

She lives and works out of her home in the beautiful English countryside, spends her spare time reading, watching films, and enjoying time with her family.

The last time she had a week's break from writing she didn't like it one little bit and has yet to meet a box of chocolates she couldn't defeat.

www.rjscott.co.uk | rj@rjscott.co.uk

NEWSLETTER - rjscott.co.uk/rjnews

facebook.com/author.rjscott

x.com/Rjscott_author

instagram.com/rjscott_author

amazon.com/author/rj-scott

bookbub.com/authors/rj-scott

goodreads.com/rjscott

pinterest.com/rjscottauthor

Also By VL Locey

For a full list of ebooks and links please scan the code above or
visit vllocey.com/stories-from-vl-locey

Meet V.L. Locey

V.L. Locey loves worn jeans, yoga, belly laughs, walking, reading and writing lusty tales, Greek mythology, the New York Rangers, comic books, and coffee.

(Not necessarily in that order.)

She shares her life with her husband, her daughter, one dog, two cats, a flock of assorted domestic fowl, and two Jersey steers.

When not writing spicy romances, she enjoys spending her day with her menagerie in the rolling hills of Pennsylvania with a cup of fresh java in hand.

vllocey.com
vicki@vllocey.com

Newsletter - vllocey.com/newsletter

facebook.com/V.L.Locey
x.com/vllocey
instagram.com/vl_locey
bookbub.com/authors/v-l-locey
goodreads.com/vllocey
pinterest.com/vllocey